P ADAMS

D1603726

TRAGG'S CHOICE

**Center Point
Large Print**

**This Large Print Book carries the
Seal of Approval of N.A.V.H.**

ॐ श्री गणेशाय नमः

CLIFTON ADAMS

TRAGG'S CHOICE

CENTER POINT PUBLISHING
THORNDIKE, MAINE

This Center Point Large Print edition
is published in the year 2002 by arrangement with
Golden West Literary Agency.

The text of this Large Print edition is unabridged. In other
aspects, this book may vary from the original edition. Printed in
Thailand. Set in 16-point Times New Roman type by
Bill Coskrey and Gary Socquet.

ISBN 1-58547-233-6

Library of Congress Cataloging-in-Publication Data.

Adams, Clifton.
    Tragg's choice / Clifton Adams.--Center Point large print ed.
        p. cm.
    ISBN 1-58547-233-6 (lib. bdg. : alk. paper)
    1. Large type books. I. Title.

PS3551.D34 T43 2002
813'.54--dc21

2002024633

CHAPTER ONE

BARSTOW had been lying beneath the mesquite tree for two days when Morrasey found him. For two days Barstow had prayed feverishly for someone, anyone, to come along and notice him. He knew only too well that his leg was broken and that gangrene had already set in. He knew that he was burned out with fever and stood almost no chance of lasting another day without help. Never had he wanted so much to see a human face, hear a human voice. . . . But he hadn't counted on anyone like Morrasey.

Even from a distance there was something about Morrasey that smacked of doom. He appeared quite suddenly atop a sand hill some hundred yards away. Barstow shouted, his voice dry and rasping. Morrasey stood there on the sand hill, cast against the dazzling sky like some gangling scarecrow. Barstow shouted again. "For God's sake, help me!"

The figure remained motionless. There was no doubt he had seen Barstow and must have known the man's condition was desperate, but several long minutes passed before he began to move. Striding down the sand hill in the loose-hipped, loping gait of a sodbuster, he sank from sight in one of those prairie arroyos and then reappeared again much nearer. It was then Barstow's sense of elation deserted him.

As desperately as Barstow needed help, he could feel no comfort in the approach of this man. Morrasey came on up to the gnarled mesquite and dropped a tow-sack bundle that he had been carrying. "Thank God," Barstow said huskily, doing his best to put enthusiasm into the words. "I been here two days. Thought I was a goner sure."

Morrasey looked at him without emotion. He wiped his sweaty face on his sleeve, then drew a piece of cable-twist tobacco from his pocket and bit off a small piece.

"I'd be much obliged for a drink of water," Barstow said weakly. "There's the river just the other side of that next sand hill. You must of seen it as you come up."

Morrasey still did not speak. He chewed for perhaps a full minute, then spat from the side of his mouth and wiped his tobacco-stained lips with the back of his hand. Sodbuster, Barstow thought to himself. That wasn't so good. Everything about Barstow said "cowman," the natural enemy of squatter farmers everywhere.

Still, Barstow reasoned, they were men, not wolves. It did not occur to him that Morrasey could refuse to make him as comfortable as he could and then go after help. "Snake spooked my horse," he explained. "That's how come I landed here with a busted leg. Good thing you come along when you did . . ." Until now he hadn't got around to wondering what Morrasey was doing afoot in the middle of the prairie. "You din't lose your animal, too, did you?"

"Never had one," Morrasey said flatly.

Barstow stared up at that rawboned, leathery face with the washed-out eyes and small, downturned mouth. It was the face of poverty and ignorance and failure. Barstow had seen it many times before, the face of the sodbuster who had foolishly thought to grow profitable crops in gravel and red clay.

"Fort Reno's over to the east somewheres," Barstow said. "I know some of the officers. There's an Army surgeon by the name of McFee. I hate to ask you to go out of your way, but . . ."

Barstow probed the depths of those washed-out eyes. They were empty. There was no feeling in them, no emotion. The cowman cleared his gravelly throat. "I wouldn't ask you to make the trip for nothin'. I'd be proud to make it worth your trouble."

The injured man held his breath. Offering to pay a cowman for an act of simple decency would have been an insult of the worst kind. He had gambled that this sodbuster would not be so sensitive about such things. And he had judged his man correctly.

Morrasey hunkered down in the lacy shade of the mesquite. His eyes were narrow, thoughtful slits. "Must be twenty miles to Reno. What you reckon it'd be worth if I went and fetched the doc?"

". . . Twenty dollars."

Morrasey rocked back on his heels. His bib overalls and collarless shirt were slick with accumulated grime. His heavy plowshoes were cracked and mended in many places. "Twenty miles is a long ways."

"Twenty dollars is a lot of money." More money than a sodbuster would likely see all together in a lifetime, and Barstow knew it.

But it was Barstow, not Morrasey, who would soon die unless he got a doctor. The sodbuster pursed his thin lips and spat a stream of tobacco juice into the gravel inches from Barstow's face. He grinned. "Fifty dollars."

The cowman made himself choke down the gall-bitter

anger. With his life at stake it was ridiculous to haggle over dollars. "All right, fifty."

By this time Morrasey was definitely interested. In the pale depths of those eyes there was the broken-glass glitter of greed. "How do I know you ain't tryin' to pull somethin'? Where do you aim to get the money?"

"Never mind. You'll get it when you bring the doctor."

Morrasey laughed abruptly, harshly. "Now that would be a fool thing for me to do. If I was to bring the doc first, there wouldn't be no reason for you to pay me anything at all."

Barstow closed his eyes and tried to keep his thoughts calm.

"Twenty now," he said. "The rest when I see the doc." He knew without a doubt that if he gave Morrasey the whole amount he'd never see him again.

Morrasey's bony jaw worked thoughtfully as he rocked on his heels. "Fair enough," he said at last.

"Now," Barstow asked bitterly, "do you think you could get me a drink of water?"

"I guess." Morrasey hauled himself to his feet. He stepped over Barstow's injured leg and started toward the line of sand hills that marked the north bank of the Cimarron. As soon as he dropped below Barstow's line of sight he reversed directions and made again for the mesquite tree.

This time he came up behind the cowman. He stood there on a gravelly ridge for several minutes watching in fascination. Barstow had unbuttoned his shirt and was working at the flaps of a money belt that he wore next to his body. Morrasey's eyes bugged when he saw the thick deck of greenbacks.

Barstow heard the sound of breathing behind him. The shallow, wolflike panting. He turned his head quickly and stared at the sodbuster. At that moment everything was painfully clear. As soon as he saw Morrasey's face, Barstow knew that he would never live to see Doc McFee or anybody else.

"I forgot to take anything to fetch the water in," Morrasey said, his hungry eyes on the money that the cowman was trying to stuff back into his belt. From his tow-sack grip he took a battered granite cup. "I'll be back in a little while." He tramped off, his big brogans crunching gravel, until he was once again out of sight of the cowman.

Morrasey took another chew of tobacco and hunkered down beneath a catclaw mesquite. Thoughtfully, he eyed the blazing sun. "Hot," he said aloud. "Won't last long, the shape he's in. Busted leg goin' bad." He tugged his greasy hat down on his forehead, closed his eyes to shut out the glare, and settled down to wait. In a vague, disinterested way, he wondered where Barstow had got all that money. Must be a hundred dollars, he guessed.

Just the thought of it almost took his breath away. In his whole life he had probably never had more than a hundred dollars cash money. He had known whole years in which he had not seen a single dollar. He wondered what Delly would say when he laid that belt out for her, showed her that thick bundle of greenbacks.

The heat in this sun-blasted river valley was stupefying. Morrasey rocked back and forth on his heels, not thinking of anything in particular. He was merely waiting, passing time. After a while he began to grunt a tune that he heard once at a country fiddling.

. . . I killed a man, they say
I beat him on the head
And left him there for dead
Yes, I left him there for dead
Goddamn his eyes!

It was only a song that he had heard at a fiddling. Hard to believe it looking at him now, but Morrasey had once been a very credible dancer. He and Delly. Not many barns in southwest Kansas that he hadn't do-si-doed in at one time or other, in his younger days. All join hands. Promenade. He could almost hear the fiddles wailing.

Well, maybe those days would come again. After he got that money. Lord, he thought to himself, it's been such a powerful long spell! So long since he'd even dared think about fiddling and dances and play parties. So long since he'd come home with a piece of bright bolt goods for Delly to sew into a dress.

Once he thought he heard Barstow shouting. But he didn't look up or open his eyes or do anything at all. There wasn't a thing in the world that anybody could do for that cowman. Doc or no doc, he was good as dead.

It wasn't that Morrasey enjoyed seeing other folks suffer. It had been in his mind to go down to the river and get the water, like Barstow wanted. But then he had thought to himself: it'll only drag it out. And it won't help. There wasn't anything in God's world that was going to save that cowman.

And when he's dead, Morrasey reasoned, that money ain't goin' to help him then. Best somebody takes it that needs it. "And Lord knows," he muttered aloud, "I sure can't think of a soul in all this world that needs it more'n Frank Morrasey!"

He sat for a long while thinking nothing. At last he spit out his worn-out cud and walked down to the river and rinsed out his mouth and drank his fill and washed his face. He decided the best thing to do was not to think about Barstow at all. After all, it wasn't as if Barstow meant anything to him. He was just a cowman. And there never was a cowman that was any account. Morrasey had plenty of reason to know all about that.

He sighed. Only thing to do, he told himself, was let nature take its course. Morrasey's conscience was clear.

Morrasey could not think of himself as a killer. He had never killed anyone in his life. Never even thought of such a thing. Hell, he thought indignantly, I never even *touched* that cowman. It ain't *my* fault that a snake spooked his horse, or that he landed the way he did and busted his leg!

He drank some more of the cool water. He sat for a long while there on the sandy bank of the Cimarron, staring at the sun-browned prairie to the south. Delly would be surprised to see him back so early. He didn't like leaving her by herself, but there had been nothing else for it. There had been no rain in Texas that spring. The cotton had come up yellow and wilted-looking, and most of the corn hadn't even sprouted. They had agreed that he would have to strike north and work the fields for other farmers and hope to raise enough money to see them through to another spring.

Now all that was changed. Or soon would be. He'd be home early, and maybe with a piece of bright bolt goods to boot. It would be good being back with Delly again.

The sun, it seemed to Morrasey, took an inordinately long time to find the western horizon. But finally it lay there on the edge of the prairie, like a sullen, smoldering coal. For the past hour or more the sodbuster's ears had been tuned to catch any sound out of the usual—but there was nothing. Only the subdued muttering of a family of plovers and the scurrying of small nocturnal things as they ventured out in time to catch the last of the sun's dying warmth.

Morrasey was peevishly angry to find Barstow still alive when he returned to the mesquite tree. But the yellow mask of death was beginning to settle on the cowman's face. Barstow worked his mouth, but Morrasey couldn't make out what he was saying. "What is it?" he asked in irritation. He stepped closer to the cowman and bent over. Barstow spoke again. It was an obscenity.

Morrasey drew himself erect, flushed and indignant. "It wasn't *me* that spooked your horse and busted your leg!"

Barstow was awkwardly tugging at his clothing with one hand. At first Morrasey didn't understand what he was trying to do. Never in his life had Frank Morrasey ever worn a revolver; he did not think in terms of firearms. When Barstow had been unhorsed, his .45 had been twisted around behind him. Now he was trying to reach it.

Morrasey kicked savagely and sent the revolver flying as the cowman worked it out of his holster. Morrasey's eyes were wide in alarm. It had not occurred to him that a man so near death might try to kill him. Well, he thought grimly, he won't be tryin' it again!

For several minutes Barstow lay perfectly still, breathing

rapidly and shallowly. He looked at Morrasey with burning eyes. "Water!"

Morrasey moved away and sat on a sand knoll. The cowman, in delirium now, appeared to be cursing the sodbuster, but Morrasey was too far away to hear. The sun sank slowly out of sight. A lingering grayness settled on the prairie. Bullbats swooped and darted, their white-striped wings flashing in the light from the other side of the horizon.

Night came down on the Cimarron. For a little while the darkness was oppressing. But after a time the pale moon seemed to move closer to the prairie, and stars by the millions glittered like ice.

Morrasey watched indifferently as a family of coyotes loped from sand hill to sand hill, appearing briefly in stark relief against a blue-black sky.

"Sodbuster!"

Morrasey was startled to hear the word spoken so loudly and, moved by curiosity, he got up and walked to the cowman. "What is it?"

"Goddamn you."

Morrasey grinned faintly, remembering the song. Goddamn your eyes!

He struck a match and held it in front of the cowman's face. Barstow was dead. "And took long enough about it too," Morrasey complained, as he began unfastening the money belt.

Morrasey, comfortably aware of the money belt around his middle, methodically went through the dead cowman's pockets, keeping anything that he could use. Knife, matches, silver coins. Not being a "gunman," he did not bother with the gun belt or revolver.

"Too bad the animal got away," he said to himself. "I sure could of used a good ridin' animal."

He walked off a few paces to where he couldn't see the body and tried to organize his thoughts. Curiously, the most difficult thing at the moment was getting used to having money. No more walking all the time, tryin' to catch rides with peddlers and tinkers. No more feeling that everybody looked down on him because he was unable to pay his way. No *more* of that!

He realized with some surprise that he was trembling with excitement. Settle down, he told himself. Get everything straight in your mind. One thing sure, the money was not going to do him any good here in the middle of the prairie. He had to find a place where it would buy something. A horse, or passage on a stage. A hat for himself. A dress for Delly.

Morrasey struck some matches and began to count the money in the belt. There was almost two hundred dollars. *Two hundred dollars!* He found two bits of paper in the belt with the money and he studied these briefly by flaring match light.

All Morrasey knew about education was from one winter in a subscription schoolhouse in Kansas, but he could read well enough to know that one of the papers was a copy of a bill of sale. It was made out by Barstow to an outfit called the Southern Missouri Packing Company. The other paper was a copy of a receipt for 190 dollars.

Well, it didn't matter now where the money had come from. Barstow was in no shape to spend it, Morrasey was.

Maybe, he thought, it was the Lord's way of evening the score for all the injustices that Morrasey had suffered at the hands of cowmen like Barstow.

He walked on with no definite plan in mind, his head still in a whirl at the thought of the great wealth which was now his. At last he sat down to rest and eat a piece of corn bread that he had begged that morning from a family of squatters in the Cherokee Outlet. He must have walked twenty miles since then, from the time he left the squatters to the time he met Barstow. Just walking and looking for work. He had been to Kansas, and the leased outfits in the Cherokee country, and the squatter places in the Panhandle. Nobody wanted a farm hand. It was a dry year, all the sodbusters were having a hard time of it.

Strange, he thought, the way things change. Just that morning he hadn't had a hope in the world. Look at him now! Thinking about new hats and dresses!

Of course, the thought continued, things change for everybody. They sure changed for Barstow.

Morrasey ate the last of his corn bread. He tore up the bill of sale and the cash receipt and threw them away. What he had to think about was getting to Delly and telling her about his good fortune. They would leave that place of gravel and clay down on the Colorado. Just get up and leave it, shack and all. Go someplace where it rained sometimes and the seeds didn't have to push rocks out of the way for a chance to look at the sun.

He wasn't sure just where he was. Somewhere between Kansas and the Texas Panhandle, in that buffer strip of appalling flat prairie known as No Man's Land. What I best do, he decided, is keep on to the west, make for the

Jones and Plummer. Catch myself a stage down to the Colorado. The only other way was to walk, and he had had his fill of that.

CHAPTER TWO

TRAGG and the Ross woman boarded the stage in Dodge City. Callahan, who had been lounging with elaborate unconcern in front of the stage office, bought a ticket just in time to catch the coach before it pulled out. Ernie Nash caught the stage, but just barely, at the shipping pens outside of town.

From time to time, at various stations and side roads along the way, other passengers would board or leave the coach, but these four were the only ones to go all the way to Beaver Station in No Man's Land. They made the trip straight through, in three eight-hour runs.

There was nothing unusual in this; many long-distance passengers preferred to take their punishment in concentrated doses rather than string it out over a period of days. The only notable thing about these passengers was that after twenty-four hours of being jostled together in close quarters, none of them had spoken a single word by way of casual conversation.

On one occasion, a short distance out of Dodge, Owen Tragg had asked Jessie Ross's permission to smoke. She had grunted. Once, as the stage lurched unexpectedly, Brian Callahan had fallen against Tragg and muttered, "Pardon." Owen Tragg had nodded. For a solid twenty-four hours Ernie Nash had said nothing at all. That young man with the magnificently bloodshot eyes rolled about like some pale cadaver in one corner of the coach, deep in the dreamless sleep of the totally debauched.

At Beaver Station, which amounted to a pole corral, a feed and harness shed, and a half dugout cabin, the passengers disembarked for a brief rest. They washed their faces in a tin basin beside the cabin door, lathering with lye soap and drying on a roller towel that had seen cleaner days. Callahan, Tragg, and the Ross woman ate flapjacks, black sorghum, and dry salt meat inside the cabin. Ernie Nash staggered down to the river and was sick.

The driver stuck his head in the cabin doorway. "Still a long haul to Tascosa. The agent can feed you and bed you down on prairie feathers, if you'd rather lay over a day."

The passengers politely declined the offer. The driver tramped down to the cottonwood grove where Ernie Nash was staring glassily at the river. "What outfit you with, boy?"

Ernie Nash grinned weakly. "Double-T, down on the Colorado."

"Been in Dodge long?"

"Six days, best I can recollect. Three months on the trail we was. When we, finally hit Dodge . . ." He groaned and the driver laughed. "The trail boss, Hank Barstow, he started back soon's he sold the Double-T herd and the few head that he had of his own." Some color was returning to the cowhand's face. He looked a little less like a corpse. "Hank was the only one with any sense. Got hisself married just before the drive started. In a big hurry to get back to the little woman—no throwin' *his* money away on rotgut whisky and saloon girls."

The driver grinned. Half the cowhands that went up the

trail left all their pay in Dodge saloons and cribs and had to sell their horses to get back home. If they were lucky enough to have a horse of their own. "Boy, it may not sound like such a good notion right now, but you better go up to the cabin and get some grub."

Ernie Nash winced but nodded. He was a sandy-haired, lanky, drawling, easygoing product of his times. It seemed that Ernie Nashes were stamped out by the thousands, all according to the same pattern. "I sure do wish," he said, "that I'd had the good sense that Hank Barstow had and headed straight back to Texas."

The men had already finished their meal by the time Nash got to the cabin. Callahan had walked off a little way from the cabin and was hunkered down with his back to a cottonwood, smoking. Tragg was over by the corral looking at the horses. They did not speak to Nash. They didn't even look at him.

The agent's wife put another plate on the table and, without a word, stacked on flapjacks and side meat and coarse hominy. "Howdy," Nash said to Jessie Ross, who was seated at the end of the table. She was just barely interested enough to glance at him. "Tell you the truth," the youth said, pulling up a cane-bottomed chair, "I ain't been feelin' none too lively since pullin' out of Dodge."

The woman stabbed a piece of flapjack and put it in her mouth.

"I'm feelin' some better now, I'm proud to say."

As she chewed the leathery flapjack, Jessie Ross looked at him without interest, without expression.

"Looks good," the young cowhand said, pouring on the sorghum. "My folks come from Arkansas, but I'm Texas.

Come up the trail with the Double-T. Three months it took us. Past six days I was up in Dodge. First real big town I ever did see."

Jessie Ross swallowed her flapjack with stolid determination, as if it were medicine. The young man, now that his strong young body was throwing off the effects of poison whisky and carousing, was eager to get someone to listen to his adventures. The woman did not dislike the young cowhand, on the other hand she did not like him. She did not feel anything at all about him.

Nash, after he had choked down the first few bites, was now eating with gusto. He was as friendly as a mongrel pup. "What I ought to of done," he was saying, "is save my money and put somethin' down on a new saddle. But I never seen a place like Dodge before. You ever buck the tiger?"

She looked at him blankly.

"That's what they call playin' faro. Don't take it up, that's my advice. That's where a good part of my pay wound up, at a faro layout. Most likely it was crooked, but I was too green to know. Ma'am," he said to the agent's wife, "you reckon I could have a few more of them flapjacks and maybe another piece of that dry salt?"

In the dim light of the half-dugout it was hard to see just what the woman looked like, except that she was dark and bony and on the edge of exhaustion. In that hot, dry summer of '88 a lot of women looked like the agent's wife. Ernie Nash had heard about the big dry-up that went all the way back to '85; as a matter of fact he wasn't old enough to know much of anything else. He knew that this was what folks called "hard times," and he had heard of squatters starving to death on burnt-out claims, but he had always managed to have a job of some kind and enough to eat. When you were young and healthy that was about all that mattered.

The agent's wife grudgingly slipped another flapjack onto Nash's plate and put a small piece of fat meat beside it.

"Now that I think of it," the cowhand said, "I ain't right sure that I even told you my name. It's Ernie Nash."

Her eyes seemed not quite in focus. Ernie wasn't sure that she had heard him. "Used to be a pack of Nashes up in Arkansas," he said, "but my folks was determined to give Texas a try. You mind if I ask your name, ma'am?"

After an uncomfortably long silence she said, "It's Jessie Ross."

"I knowed a Ross once, Gramma Ross that had a little shack up on Peachtree Creek in Arkansas. That's where they fought the big battle when the war was goin' on. You meetin' up with your husband somewheres?"

Jessie Ross said nothing.

"Reason I ask is so many folks movin' here and there nowadays. Whole world unsettled, looks like. On account of the hard times, I guess."

"I don't have a husband."

"Oh." The young man mopped his plate clean and sat back and patted his stomach. He picked his teeth with a matchstick and looked about for coffee. But there wasn't any coffee. In a comfortably abstracted way he gazed around at the drab little cabin and gradually let his attention settle on Jessie Ross.

He was surprised to discover that the woman was

nowhere near as old as he had thought, and in fact she was very little, if any, older than Ernie himself. This, he decided, was due to the fact that she never seemed to smile, and in her eyes there was a curious dullness that youth usually associates with old age. Ernie began to suspect that she had remained in her chair, listening to his talk, not because she wished to hear anything he had to say, but because she simply didn't care enough to get up and leave.

"Tell you the truth," Ernie went on—he was one of those people who simply like to talk, and it didn't really make much difference whether anybody listened. "Tell you the truth, I never rode a coach before, except a few miles at a time, from Bosen's Grove to Tanglefoot. If you don't mind, I think maybe I'll tramp around some and try to get the kinks out of my back."

Obviously Jessie Ross did not mind. Ernie politely touched the crimped brim of his hat and pushed back his chair.

In the grip of inertia, Jessie Ross continued to sit at the table after Ernie Nash had gone. The agent's wife cleared the table and wearily began to scrape the dishes. It won't be long, Jessie thought, before I look like that. The prairie and hard times. That's what they did to a woman. Sometimes it seemed that all the women west of Kansas City had been formed in the same grim mold. Coly used to go on about how pretty she was—but she wasn't pretty any more. The drying wind, the heat, too much work, and not enough food. That young cowhand . . . he was the kind who would ride all day for the opportunity to make calf eyes at some nester girl at a camp meeting or country dance. She had seen the way he looked at her, the surprise in his eyes. All the time he had been assuming that she was a woman nearing middle age, and he was startled to suddenly discover that she was much younger.

Of course, it didn't matter what that cowhand thought about her—and yet he had, in a way, proved Coly right. "It happens before you know it," Coly had told her. "My ma died when she was thirty-four. She looked sixty. Get away while you got the chance, Jessie."

That's what she was doing. Getting away.

Brian Callahan was lounging against the trunk of a live-oak tree, gazing flatly out at the small stream that cut through the dry heart of No Man's Land. Here in the creek bottom the country was green and inviting, the only decent farmland that Callahan had seen for days. But it was contested land. There was no way of getting title to it and no way to stake a legal claim. In the eye of Callahan's mind he could see an ocean of wheat rippling with the wind—at some future time. Maybe when folks didn't need it so much.

From time to time the gall would rise in his throat and he would have to choke it down. Once Callahan himself had tried to work a claim in the Oklahoma country. But the soldiers had driven him out. It was all right, it seemed, for Texas cowmen to graze their cattle on Indian land, but farmers were not welcome. Well, he thought to himself, quietly, coldly, if they would not let a man be a farmer, then he would be something else.

Callahan was a large, balding man with a florid face and coarse features. In the past he had tried many things besides farming. He had cut and hauled timber in the

Choctaw Nation. He had served with the Indian fighting army in Arizona. He had worked for the railroads as a strikebreaker. He was a man with a consuming hunger and little talent for satisfying it. But it was just possible that he had finally found his calling.

"Howdy," Ernie Nash said, grinning.

Callahan turned and glanced at the cowhand coolly.

"Got myself some grub," the cowhand went on with irrepressible friendliness. "Proud to say I'm in better shape now than I was back at Dodge. Wonder how much farther it is to Tascosa?"

"Ask the agent."

The young man shrugged. "Don't make any difference. We'll get there when we get there. You goin' all the way?"

Callahan said nothing. Apparently the young cowhand was used to being ignored, for it did not seem to bother him. "Come up the trail with the Double-T," he told Callahan. "All the way from Colorado. Took us three months. You ever been up the trail?"

"No."

"Lightnin'," Ernie Nash said with the sober air of an expert. "Worst thing there is. Surprises you some, don't it? She's a fact, though. Lightnin' causes more stampedes and commotion than anything you can think of."

Callahan started to walk away. The cowhand fell in beside him, still talking. "Hank Barstow, our trail boss, was the only one of the bunch with any sense. Soon's he sold the herd he started back to Texas. Had a few head of his own and sold them too. Give him a nest egg to take back to the little woman. Hank," he added confidentially, "got hisself hitched just before we hit the trail."

Callahan was profoundly uninterested in Nash's experiences on the trail, but there seemed no way of getting rid of him without making a fuss. They walked toward the corral where the driver and agent were hitching up fresh horses. Callahan asked in a casual tone, "You haven't got around to talkin' to Tragg, have you?"

"Ain't felt much like talkin' to anybody till now."

"Interestin' kind of bird," Callahan said, drawing a stubby little Louisiana crook from his vest pocket and lighting it. "Used to be famous. I remember seein' his picture on the front of *Harper's Weekly* once."

The cowhand's eyes brightened. "Famous?"

"You heard about Jody Barker, ain't you?"

"The famous gunslinger? The outlaw?"

Callahan nodded. "That old bird over there by the corral is Owen Tragg. The one that killed Jody Barker."

"I'll be damned." The cowhand stared. "He don't look like much, does he? I mean, for the one that killed Jody Barker."

Callahan laughed. "That was some years ago."

"I guess. You know what he puts me in mind of? A medicine show doctor."

Callahan laughed again. It was a dry, mechanical sound, devoid of mirth. Tragg wasn't a medicine show doctor—not yet—but he wasn't much above it.

"Wonder where he got that rig?" Ernie Nash said in wonder.

"Why don't you go over and ask him?"

Owen Tragg had once been painfully aware of the ridiculous figure that he cut. But the lecture manager had insisted, "Tragg, you got to give folks somethin' to look at and talk about. What difference does it make if they laugh at you? Just so they notice you. That's the thing that sells tickets."

At first Tragg had resisted. His manager had reminded him, "Look, Tragg, folks has got lots on their minds nowadays. Indian troubles, closin' the cattle trails, openin' the Oklahoma country. Damn few people recollect Jody Barker, much less the deputy marshal that killed him. And you might as well face it, you ain't no Wild Bill Hickok when it comes to puttin' on a show."

So, in the end, the lecture manager had his way. He had fitted Owen out in a buckskin hunting shirt with fancy Indian beadwork and nine-inch tassels from shoulder to wrist, buckskin pants with more tassels and beadwork, and a special-made hat heavy with still more beads and silver conchos. He was eternally amazed that the audience didn't roll on the floor with laughter the instant he walked on the stage in that outfit. For some reason they never did. It was the way they seemed to expect a former deputy U.S. marshal to dress. Even when he became less popular and the lecture moved west where people knew better, they rarely laughed. Now he had worn the outfit for so long that he seldom thought about it.

"Marshal Tragg?"

Owen turned and looked at the young cowhand. Ernie Nash was staring at him in innocent awe. People used to come up to him and stare because he was Owen Tragg; now they did it because of the way he looked.

On that day ten years ago, when Owen had knelt over Jody Barker and watched him die, he had looked much like any other marshal riding for the court at Fort Smith. Clean-shaven, thirty-five, beginning to thicken in the middle. Now he was a little thicker at the middle. His hair, growing down to his shoulders, was going gray. The beard that the lecture manager had insisted on was a neatly trimmed spike, the mustaches drooping at the corners of his mouth in the manner once favored by cavalry officers. "You still ain't no Hickok or Cody," the manager had told him, "but you do look a *little* more the way a U.S. marshal ought to look."

That, Owen remembered, was long ago. Jody Barker had been in his grave for ten years.

"I guess you're goin' to think I'm some kind of a fool, Marshal," Ernie Nash was saying soberly. "I mean, bein' in the coach together all this time and not even knowin' who you are."

"No reason why you should."

"That ain't right," the young man said, completely serious. "Everybody's heard about the man that killed Jody Barker. I aimed to go and hear your lecture in Dodge City, but what with one thing and another . . ."

Owen smiled faintly. It was a brutal fact that he could have used another customer or two in the audience. Dodge had been the end of the line as far as lectures were concerned. His manager had collected his last commission and had taken the next train to Kansas City. "Face up to it, Tragg. Folks ain't interested any longer in the man that killed Jody Barker." There was a small circus in Kansas City with a dog act that needed a manager. That was the last Owen had seen of him.

"Might be," the cowhand was saying, "I'll get to hear

you in Tascosa."

"I won't be givin' the lecture in Tascosa."

Nash looked disappointed. "It ain't much of a place, I guess."

That wasn't what Owen had meant. He was glad to hear the driver calling, " 'Board for Tascosa," and save him the trouble of explaining.

They settled themselves in the coach, Tragg and Callahan facing to the rear, the cowhand and Jessie Ross facing to the front, the padded jump bench in between. The driver called down from the box, "We'll make good time rest of the way to Tascosa, barrin' flash floods and dust storms. We'll run right through the night, but the country's flat and the road ain't bad, so maybe you can get yourselves some sleep. There'll be a change of horses over the Texas line, if some of you wants to stretch your legs."

"What time you due in Tascosa?" Callahan asked.

"When we get there," the driver said dryly. "Tascosa's the end of the regular mail run. If you want to go on south or west you'll have to catch whatever rig that happens to be goin' that way. Ever'body set?"

The passengers took firm holds on their tug straps and the coach lurched away from Beaver Station.

Ernie Nash, swinging loosely from his bit of leather, chattered aimlessly as the stage started its gradual ascent to the High Plains. Only once did Jessie Ross give any indication that she had heard anything he said. He had leaned over until he was touching her shoulder and said, with an air of mystery, "See the old bird across from me? You know who he is?"

Jessie Ross glanced at Tragg and shrugged.

"Owen Tragg. The U.S. marshal that killed Jody Barker."

He was surprised and gratified at Miss Ross's sudden show of interest. She shot a quick glance at the bearded face, the tired eyes. "You sure?"

"Sure I'm sure. I talked to him just before the stage pulled away from Beaver Station."

Her show of interest lasted only a moment. Then she turned her attention to the monotonous stretches of prairie that rushed beneath the wheels of the coach.

It was midafternoon when they stopped to rest and water the horses. "Got another passenger for you," the agent said as the rugged Concord rattled to a stop.

A lanky, rawboned figure stooped through the doorway of the agent's sod hut. Morrasey opened the stage door and grinned in at the passengers. "Reckon there's always room for one more, like they say." He handed his tow sack up to the driver and got in.

"Name's Morrasey," he told them, ignoring the center bench and wedging himself in beside Ernie Nash. "Frank Morrasey. Be ridin' with you all the way down to the Colorado—if any of you're goin' that far."

The passengers looked at him but no one spoke, not even Nash.

All right, Morrasey thought bitterly, if the bunch of you want to be uppity, it don't matter to me. He didn't need anything from them. He was paying his own way.

He sourly regarded the masklike faces of his companions. Go ahead, he told them silently, and look smug, if it makes you feel better. Don't think I can't see what you're thinkin'. Wonderin' what a poor ragged sodbuster's doin' ridin' with the payin' passengers.

But if he could have looked into their heads he would have seen that they weren't thinking about him at all, except in passing, and with an undefined distaste.

There was a moment, when he first entered the coach, that the young cowhand had looked at him in a certain way, almost in recognition. "Howdy," Nash said finally in his friendly way.

Morrasey nodded. "Howdy."

"Name's Ernie Nash," the cowhand said with a faintly puzzled frown. "This lady here's Miss Ross. Over there's Mr. Callahan and Marshal Tragg."

Morrasey looked at them and nodded. "Marshall Tragg," Nash went on, as unstoppable as a flash flood in spring-time, "is the one that killed Jody Barker some time back."

Morrasey looked at Tragg with interest. Although he had never heard of Jody Barker, he experienced an instant fascination for one who had killed another man, for whatever reason. Brian Callahan lay back on the black leather seat and smiled faintly at Tragg's discomfort.

With the inevitable whoop, the coach lurched away from the station, and the passengers clung grimly to their tug straps until the first gaudy show of leave-taking was over and the driver paced his team for the long haul ahead. Now the coach swayed gently as the seemingly endless stretches of tableland slipped past the window. Shock from the rutted mail road was absorbed in the heavy thorough bracing of New Hampshire coachwork. The passengers were crowded but reasonably comfortable. Dust, as long as they headed into the wind, was no problem.

The monotony of Panhandle travel was stupefying to

most of them. The spaces were too huge for the human mind to comfortably consider. The emptiness of the High Plains, the dazzling blue of the endless sky somehow caused a man to shrivel inside. It left him feeling as hollow as a winter gourd. It gave him an ache of loneliness in his gut when he looked at it too long.

One by one the passengers closed their reddened eyes and dozed. Even Ernie Nash stopped rambling about his experiences on the trail and slumped down in the seat and was soon sleeping on Jessie Ross's shoulder. Each traveler retreated into the private world of his mind.

Owen Tragg's secret world was composed of two recurring nightmares. The first was of Jody Barker staring at him with the hot, fierce eyes of the dying who knew they were dying. *"You promised, Tragg—you promised to a dyin' man!"* The other nightmare had its setting in St. Louis, in a famous opera house. And the opera house was filled with people, and a storm of hand clapping and whistling and stomping rolled like an all-destroying tidal wave toward the small, ridiculous figure on the stage. In later days his sense of panic and shame became blunted to where he scarcely noticed it, but in the nightmare it was always new and sharp and bitter. He could still feel the sweat flowing in cold rivulets down his back, soaking his fancy outfit of buckskin and tassels.

Frank Morrasey's secret world, until recently, had been a state of vague, hopeless wishing for something better. Something for himself and Delly, and for the children, if they ever had any. Sometimes it would bubble in his blood like poison, but most of the time it was a natural part of him, like his skin or his filthy overalls. A nagging chronic hunger for something better than parched corn for coffee, and a belly that was never quite full, and a wife slowly dying before his eyes, wasting away. But that, he thought with sudden viciousness, was all over now. He had money! His luck had turned!

Jessie Ross also knew what it was to wish for something better, with no hope of ever getting it. Then she had met Coly Brown. Young and violent and gay, Coly had uprooted her and taught her what a fine thing it was to hear laughter. With laughter and passion and, she guessed, love, he had wrenched her free of the prairie homestead where her parents had worked themselves to the edge of madness and starvation.

Jessie smiled to herself. The places they had gone! The things they had done and seen together! She and the violent young Coly Brown!

The smile froze, then vanished without a trace. The wild and happy days with Coly were over. Every turn of the coach's wheels, every thud of the horses' hoofs, widened the distance between her and Coly. She would never see him again. Get away, he had said, it's the only chance you'll ever have. And here she was, in a land even more desolate than the one she had left. I wonder, she thought to herself, if Coly's dead?

Ernie Nash's secret world was as innocent as his waking one. He dreamed contentedly of friends who had come with him up the trail, of the comfortable and satisfying wickedness of Dodge City cribs and saloons, of a certain nester girl down on the Colorado, of line camps and roundups and familiar faces. He was young and uncomplicated. He was returning from an unforgettable experience without a horse of his own but not without his saddle—as long as he could manage that, he had nothing serious to worry about.

His chin resting on his chest, Brian Callahan gave the impression of sleeping while he was actually watching Jessie Ross with great interest. All the time they had been in the coach together Callahan had done no more than grunt to the woman. But she had been very much in his thoughts. He had been especially elated when he had seen the brief smile tilt the corners of her mouth. That's right, my girl, he thought happily. Think about Coly Brown. Then he sat comfortably back against the black leather and closed his eyes and slept.

CHAPTER THREE

TASCOSA was a raw new town at the end of the main mail road from Dodge City. A few years ago this had been buffalo country. The main war trail of the Comanches had come through here, going all the way to Chihuahua. But now the Comanches were on the reservation and the cowmen had claimed the country for their own. To the east was Mobeetie and the Old Mobeetie Road that extended into Indian Territory. To the west was the dreaded Llano Estacado, and to the south, along the Colorado, more cattle and a scattering of nesters. Tascosa was a hub from which several trails and roads spoked out, each toward its own peculiar wasteland.

The town itself was a cluster of huts, some of sod and some of poorly cured adobe. Like most cow towns, there was a depressing feeling of impermanence about the place.

It was only a few years old and already gave the impression that it was dying of old age.

And so it was. Within a few years it would be gone. Jessie Ross, with her woman's eyes, could see this more clearly than the others. She stood beside the stage depot listening to the whooping and laughter, and she sensed that before long all those wild young men would be scattered, and the town would be as dead as the crumbling old fort to the north, the place called Adobe Walls.

Without turning her head, she knew that Callahan was watching her. He had been watching her, without appearing to, from the time he first entered the stage in Dodge City. It was attention that she did not want, but it did not overly disturb her. She had been stared at before. There goes Coly Brown's woman, they would say. But, like Callahan, they always kept their distance. When you belonged to a man like Coly you didn't have to worry about being bothered by others.

Most of the passengers had gathered aimlessly in front of the sod stage office, waiting for the agent to get their grips out of the rear boot. Morrasey, his bony jaws working his tobacco cud, spat into the red dust and called to the driver, "How long before a stage takes us on towards Bosen's Grove?"

"Ain't no stage to Bosen's Grove," the driver informed him. "There'll be a mud wagon that way sometime tomorrow."

"Tomorrow?" There was dismay in Jessie Ross's voice.

"You're runnin' in luck, ma'am," the driver told her blandly. "That mud wagon don't run but maybe ever' week or ten days." He jammed his hands in his pockets and went off to find a saloon.

Callahan was at her elbow the instant the agent handed down her carpet valise. "Can I help you with that, ma'am?"

She studied his face for a moment, but it was as blank as an Indian dance mask. "I can manage," she told him, picking up the valise and lugging it awkwardly to the office. Owen Tragg was just coming out of the sod hut, and on impulse she said, "Marshal, can I talk to you a minute?"

He didn't look surprised. For almost ten years he had been having perfect strangers coming up to him, wanting to talk to him about one thing or another—usually about Jody Barker. He somehow managed a smile and nodded politely. "Yes, ma'am. Can I give you a hand with your grip?"

She shook her head impatiently. "That ain't what I wanted. I heard you talkin' to the stage agent a little bit ago—I take it you're goin' on through, like some of the rest of us."

Vaguely puzzled, he nodded. "As far as El Paso. If," he said, smiling wearily, "the mud wagon gets us to Bosen's Grove. And if the coaches on the old Butterfield line still make connection there." He did not think it necessary to mention that he meant to lay over in Bosen's Grove before going on to El Paso. "It's been a long time," he added, "since I was in this part of the country."

"But you're acquainted with it."

"I used to be," he confessed.

"Could you tell me somethin' about it? I mean . . ." She looked slightly flustered. "You bein' a marshal and all, I figgered you could tell me about the courts down here. The law."

His look of puzzlement became more pronounced, but he answered her as well as he could. "Well, the country here is organized into counties, like most places. There's a sheriff, and maybe a few deputies, if anybody's got the money to pay for them. A circuit judge, in most cases, that takes the different courts in turn."

Her head bobbed up and down as he spoke. She didn't look directly at him, and there were spots of color in her cheeks. "Could I," she asked slowly, "talk to you official-like?"

"How do you mean?"

Tragg could see that the conversation was becoming difficult for her. After a silence that was becoming painfully long, she said, "You bein' a lawman and all, I got to thinkin' that maybe you could help me. And at the same time," she added, "not let it get any further than just the two of us. What we talk about."

Tragg wasn't sure how to answer her. He only knew that he was beginning not to like the direction this conversation was taking. "Ma'am," he said at last, "I haven't been a lawman for almost ten years. I think there's a marshal here in Tascosa . . ."

"It ain't a lawman I want," she said quickly. "It's just that I don't know how to go about it."

"About what, ma'am?" he asked with studied politeness.

He watched her take a deep breath, bracing herself for the plunge. "What I aim to say is, I don't know just how I would go about collectin' the bounty."

Tragg, during the years of riding for a federal court, had seen bounty hunters in many shapes and sizes, but he had never come across one just like Jessie Ross.

"Bounty?" he asked quietly.

"There's somebody I know—he killed a man. That's what they say, anyhow. There's a reward, but I don't know . . ." Suddenly she showed all of her emotions in one brief outburst. "After all I've been through, I don't aim for some sharpshooter to do me out of what's rightly mine!"

Tragg asked in the same quiet tone, "You know where the fugitive's hidin'?"

She nodded miserably. Tragg, sensing that there was something more here than the clear-cut act of betrayal that he had encountered so many times before, resisted the temptation to turn on his heel and walk away. "If the reward's out," he said, "and you know where the fugitive is, I'm afraid I don't understand the problem."

"I ain't right sure where I ought to go to get the money. I'm afraid there's folks that would try to do me out of it."

The conviction was growing in Tragg's mind that he ought to let things stand just where they were—if it wasn't already too late. All the same, he heard himself asking, "What's the reward posted for?"

She turned her gaze toward the rowdy mud huts of Tascosa. ". . . Murder." After a moment she added, "There was a holdup. An express agent was killed. And a passenger that was in the coach at the time."

"The express company's put up the reward money? You could of saved yourself a hard trip. Any express office or county sheriff could of handled it for you."

She shook her head. "It ain't the express company. It's an old Mex sheepman down by Bosen's Grove. The passenger that got killed was his boy."

Suddenly Tragg was tired of this story and tired of this

conversation with Jessie Ross. "In that case," he said shortly, "you'll have to make your own bargain with the sheepman." With a rudeness that was foreign to his nature, he abruptly touched his hatbrim. "Good day, Miss Ross."

"Marshal." She spoke quickly as he started to turn away. "Marshal, is it a bargain between the two of us? What I said about the bounty . . . ?"

"It's just between the two of us, Miss Ross," he said dryly. With another curt gesture of parting, he turned toward the town.

Ernie Nash, grinning self-consciously, appeared at Jessie's side. "Sure ain't much, is it? After Dodge. You give any thought yet to where you're goin' to spend the night?"

Jessie looked blank. She hadn't had time to think that far ahead. "Tell you what," the young cowhand said with irrepressible good humor, "you make yourself easy there in the station office, I'll see what I can find."

She nodded her thanks and the cowhand strolled off toward the nearest saloon. That was the last she saw of him until the mud wagon pulled out the next morning.

The station agent peered into the hut where Jessie was sitting and had been sitting for the past two hours. "Found yourself a place to sleep?" he asked.

"Mr. Nash's scoutin' the town now, lookin' for a hotel."

The agent laughed explosively. "That cowhand's down at the Gold Garter with his neck full of red whisky. Anyhow, he couldn't find a hotel if he was cold sober— there ain't any. Me and Ma fix up to board and sleep the passengers sometimes. Course, if you'd rather sleep here in the office . . ."

"No," she said quickly. Every bone in her body seemed

to ache. "I'd be much obliged," she told the agent, "if you could put me up for the night."

"You're smart," he grinned. "There ain't but one bunk left." He pointed with his chin. "Pick up your grip and foller me."

He led her to a sullen gray adobe but not much larger than the stage office. The inevitable washstand and lye soap and filthy towel were just outside the door. Imperfectly cured buffalo robes, strung on rawhide lines, partitioned the interior into four tiny cubicles, each cubicle just large enough to hold one grass-filled mattress. "Well," she tried to convince herself, "it's better than no place at all."

"Six bits for the night," the agent said. "Ma's fixin' supper over at the shack. That'll be another four bits, if you want it."

The shack was a plain brush arbor behind the "hotel" where the agent had set up a raw plank table and two benches. A woman, who might have been a sister to the wife of the agent at Beaver Station, wearily served pinto beans and hoecake bread to the passengers.

Jessie took a place at the head of the table. In a little while Callahan appeared and sat across from her. "Well, it ain't the fanciest grub I ever seen," he said, "but I guess it ain't the worst either." The beans had been boiled with red chilies, and after the first few bites his eyes began to water. He pulled out a blue bandanna and wiped the tears away. "I take it," he said to the young woman, "you'll be goin' south with the mud wagon."

She ate slowly, steadily, her eyes on her place.

Undisturbed, Callahan went on, "Looks like the whole bunch of us is goin' on through. Far as the Colorado, anyway. You ever been down that far, Miss Ross?"

She looked at him for the first time but didn't bother to speak. Callahan shrugged and wiped his eyes. "With any kind of luck," he continued, "we ought to make Bosen's Grove in two days."

Jessie put down her piece of greasy hoecake. "What is it you're after, Callahan?"

Suddenly he laughed. "That's what I like, a woman that says what's on her mind! But I thought you knowed all along what I was after, ma'am. That bounty that's on the head of Coly Brown."

He watched her steadily as the color drained from her face. "Leastwise," he said quietly, "that's what I *was* after. I been on Coly's trail almost two months, ever since that express holdup. I figger I just about *earned* that bounty." He tilted his head over on one thick shoulder and studied her. "I'll be honest with you, ma'am. I lost Coly's trail up by the unassigned lands, in the Chickasaw Nation. And I got to admit it was an accident when we run into each other in Dodge. Then, when I seen you buyin' a ticket on that stage, I says to myself, 'Now where you reckon Coly Brown's little woman's taken' herself off to?' And you know what answer I give myself?"

She was seized by an overpowering sense of hopelessness. Somewhere along the line she had taken the wrong fork, and it was leading her over the edge. She started to speak, then realized that there was nothing to say. Everything she had done had been for nothing.

"Why, I said to myself," he went on pleasantly, " 'Now where do you *think* Coly Brown's woman would be goin'? She'd be goin' to Coly, of course.' That makes

39

sense, don't it, Miss Ross?"

He smiled coldly when she did not answer. "It makes sense to me," he said with mock sadness. "But when the station agent in Dodge told me you was goin' straight through to Tascosa, I knowed somethin' was wrong. Everything I could find out about Coly made me think he had headed for someplace in Kansas after that holdup. But here his woman was, headed the other way." He paused meaningfully. "You know what I thought *then,* Miss Ross?"

She sat like stone, staring at Callahan but listening to another, a different, voice. I'm sorry, Coly! I'm sorry!

Callahan's tone had taken on a dry, sarcastic edge. "I know you ain't goin' to believe this, ma am. But it crossed my mind that you was settin' yourself to turn Coly in and collect that bounty yourself." He smiled. "Just goes to show what a suspicious mind I've got."

Callahan sat back slightly and beamed with sudden good humor, as if an old nagging mystery had just been made clear to him. "Well, that's that. I know all about it, and you know that I know. That kind of makes us partners, wouldn't you say, Miss Ross?"

"What do you want?" she demanded bitterly.

"Good, I'm glad we're down to cases. What I want, ma'am, is half the bounty when you collect it."

Her eyes glittered. "You're loco. I don't have to give you anything."

"Course you don't. But if you want to collect that money without Coly and his bunch knowin' who turned him in, half of that bounty is what it'll cost you."

"I won't do it!" she hissed. "I won't touch that bounty!"

"That's up to you, ma'am. I'm just sayin' if you do, I get half of it."

Morrasey appeared around the corner of the stage office and came toward them in that slouching, shambling gait of a sodbuster. He sat at the far end of the table, saying nothing, digging immediately into the beans and hoecake. Callahan nodded to Jessie Ross with excessive politeness. "Good day, ma'am. I reckon we'll be seein' one another tomorrow on the mud wagon." He pushed back from the table and strolled toward the heart of town.

Morrasey, from beneath shaggy brows, stared at the woman with sullen resentment. *Look at her. Thinks she's too good to waste the time of day on a sodbuster.* He wolfed the beans and heavy pan bread. It was galling to have folks like this snotty doxy look down her nose at him, just because she thought he was nothing and had nothing. Well, he thought savagely, it might just surprise you some if you *knew* what I had!

Morrasey raised his head briefly as Owen Tragg took a seat across from Jessie Ross. Both the woman and the marshal appeared curiously ill at ease. A terrible anger crept into Morrasey's throat as he watched them. There was no doubt in his mind that they had been talking about him, saying bad things about him, and now they were ashamed to find themselves at the same table with him.

He kept his hate-filled eyes on his food as he ate. Think about something else, he told himself. It wouldn't do any good to get himself worked up. Then he raised his head to see Owen Tragg and the woman looking at him in a disturbing way. The fancy marshal was frowning and asking quietly, "What did you say, Morrasey?"

He had been talking to himself again. It was a habit that he had got into while walking alone up and down this famine-cursed country. "Nothin'," he muttered sullenly. "I was just wonderin' . . ." Quickly he ate all the bread and beans that his stomach could comfortably hold, and then he made himself eat a few bites more. A man who had lived so long on the edge of starvation did not soon forget what it was like to be hungry.

"A strange man," Tragg said quietly, after the sodbuster had tramped angrily away from the table.

Jessie Ross appeared ill at ease and in no way concerned with Frank Morrasey. "Marshal," she said at last, "about what we was talkin' about before—I'd be much obliged if you just put it out of your mind. I . . . I've decided not to collect that bounty after all."

Tragg shot her a fleeting look. "I see." But he did not see. Something had happened since their brief talk at the stage office, but he was sure that she had not changed her mind about the bounty.

"You don't believe me?" Her tone was clearly challenging.

"It don't matter what I believe, ma'am," he said quietly. "I gave you my word that our talk was between just the two of us. I keep my word."

He saw the spots of color appear in her cheeks. She seemed about to press her point, then realized that she would only be making an awkward situation more awkward. With a curt little nod she turned her attention to her plate, and the meal was finished in silence.

An hour before sunup the passengers, puffy-eyed and

unrested, gathered at the agent's table for barley coffee, corn dogs, and black sorghum. "Coach pullin' out in ten minutes," the driver warned. "Anybody with plunder to go into the boot better see to it now."

Tragg and Jessie Ross plodded toward the mud wagon with their meager luggage. Callahan and Morrasey lingered over their coffee. Ernie Nash left the table with a groan, hoisted his sacked saddle to his hip, and stumbled blindly through the early morning darkness.

The driver lounged against the rear wheel and made no offer to help with the luggage. Tragg stowed his own grip and that of Jessie Ross in the undersized rear boot, then he helped the young cowhand wrestle the heavy saddle to the top of the coach.

"I ain't right proud to say it," the haggard young Nash confessed, "but it looks like red whisky's goin' to be the death of me, if I don't get back to the Double-T pretty soon."

Tragg grinned and gave him a boost to the seat. From Tascosa to the Colorado was going to be a very long trip, especially for Ernie Nash. For Tragg himself it would not be long enough. It was a trip that he had put off, one way and another, for ten years. Now he couldn't put it off any longer.

Jessie Ross eyed the mud wagon with open hostility. "It sure don't look like much of a rig."

"Ain't much travelin'," the driver told her, "between here and Bosen's Grove. And what there is is mostly horsebackers."

But Jessie had been undeniably right; it wasn't much of a rig. A flat bed on a set of plain running gears. Canvas top and side curtains, two spring seats behind the driver's box. Four dispirited brown mules slumped in the traces. "Well," she consoled herself wryly, "it can't be much worse than a hay mattress with bedbugs."

She was wrong. Within an hour all the passengers were exhausted from fighting the ceaseless pitching of the light vehicle as it rattled over an almost trackless prairie. Dust rose in a choking cloud, and the side curtains were no help. The heat was stupefying, the sun blinding, and after a few hours the monotony of the High Plains was almost maddening.

Jessie Ross, her face a gray mask of dust, was wedged into the rear seat beside Owen Tragg. Callahan rode beside Ernie Nash in the front seat, and Morrasey was up on the box with the driver. It was around midday when Jessie grasped Tragg's arm and gasped, "How . . . how much farther?"

Tragg glanced up at the sun. "Tonight sometime ought to put us halfway to Bosen's Grove."

"Another day of this!" Her voice was a thin wail. "I don't think I can make it!"

"You can lay over at the next station and catch a later mud wagon."

She was appalled. "If I ever stopped I don't think I'd have the nerve to start again!"

Tragg smiled faintly. He felt himself isolated—set aside from his companions—and so he was. They were anxious—almost desperate—to have this journey done with. Tragg, if he could have done so, would have stretched it out forever.

At the next station they changed teams and rested until

there was enough moonlight to drive by. Then they struck once more to the south. Shortly before dawn they stopped for another brief rest.

"Easy haul from here to Bosen's Grove," the driver assured them. "Ought to make it in time for supper today, with any kind of luck."

They were less than half a day away when their luck ran out. The front axle snapped with the report of a rifle shot. The mud wagon lurched crazily. The mules dragged it for a short distance in panic. Then a front wheel collapsed and they skidded to a violent halt.

CHAPTER FOUR

FOR several minutes all was confusion and swirling dust and a scorching blast of profanity from the driver. Ernie Nash had been thrown free of the coach and was picking himself out of a gully almost fifty yards from the place where the mud wagon finally came to a stop. Predictably, he hurried to the drastically listing hack to make sure that his saddle hadn't been damaged. Then he threw back the side curtains and asked, "Miss Ross, you all right in there?"

Owen Tragg had been thrown to the floor boards between the two seats, and Jessie Ross had fallen on top of him. Jessie glanced at the cowhand and said testily, "I'm all right. Just get me out of here."

Obligingly, Nash tore down the side curtains, flung open the door and dragged her out. "Ever'body else all right?"

Tragg, except for a cut on his forehead, found himself unhurt. Callahan had been thrown against the driver's box, but seemed to be in one piece. Morrasey had ridden the mishap out on the box alongside the driver. One of the mules was down in the traces.

"Busted foreleg," the driver announced sourly.

"Well, what're you goin' to do about it?" Morrasey demanded, as if the driver had broken the axle on purpose just to plague him.

The driver, whose name was Hugh Garden, made an impressive show of pretending that Morrasey did not exist. Garden and Ernie Nash methodically began unhitching the three sound mules. When they were free, the cowhand led them away a good distance from the wagon. The driver stood for a moment, looking down at the injured mule, and the mule, with great hurt eyes, looked back at him. "I ain't proud to do this, old son," Garden said quietly. He drew an ancient converted .44, cocked it, and gently placed the muzzle behind one tufted ear.

The explosion rocketed on the heat-laden air. Ernie Nash crooned to the other animals to gentle them. Tragg and Jessie Ross looked at each other, then away. Callahan suddenly found something of consuming interest in the monotony of the naked horizon. Only Morrasey did not look away as the downed mule kicked its last.

"I was countin' on bein' at my place by sunup tomorrow," the sodbuster complained. "It ain't no more'n right. I paid my way."

The driver looked straight through him. Then he put away the .44 and turned to Jessie Ross. He spoke to Jessie but what he said was meant for all of them. "If there was any timber in these parts we could maybe splint the axle and rig up a drag where the bad wheel is. But . . ." He turned and scanned the prairie. The nearest thing to timber was some runted thornbush, nothing much bigger than a man's finger. "You can see how it is. I'll take one of the mules and ride on to Bosen's Grove and send back a rig for you and your plunder."

"There's three mules," Morrasey was quick to point out. "Ain't no need for all of us to stay here."

The passengers discussed it for a moment. Tragg was in no hurry to get to Bosen's Grove, and neither, apparently, was Jessie Ross. Obviously Callahan was not going to let Coly Brown's woman out of his sight, if he could help it. It was agreed that Garden and Morrasey and Nash should take the mules. The others would wait with the mud wagon.

The three of them rode into the scorching heat of another day. Hugh Garden took the setback philosophically—when you drove an unscheduled mud wagon over ungraded roads you had to accustom yourself to these inconveniences. Ernie Nash, though still sour from his night in Tascosa and eager to get back to his outfit, did not complain.

Only Morrasey openly displayed his impatience and grew more ill tempered as the day went on. He sat his mule's bare back like a sack of oats, long legs dangling, muttering his displeasure to himself. His only comfort came from the leathery hug of the money belt about his middle. He closed his eyes and tried to imagine what he would do with all that money. He tried to imagine how Delly's eyes would shine when she saw it. All those greenbacks, thicker than poke greens in a creek bottom! How

Delly would laugh when he told her about the way he'd taken that money off a cowman!

"Where'd you get that?"

Morrasey blinked. Several seconds passed before he realized that the cowhand's question was directed at him. In his hand Morrasey was idly fingering a small silver concho, a shiny disk not much larger than a ten-cent piece—one of several small articles that he had taken from the dead cowman's pockets.

Ernie Nash reached out and grasped Morrasey's hackamore. "Where'd you get that?" he asked again. This time there was a decided edge to his voice. The cowhand leaned forward in his saddle and brought Morrasey's mule to a halt.

The sodbuster regarded Nash with irritation. "Let go of my mule."

"Where'd you get that concho?"

Morrasey, beginning to get angry, spat into the dirt. "I don't figger that's none of your business."

The stage driver, deep in his own thoughts, let his mule plod on for several lengths before curiosity caused him to look back. "What's the matter with you two?"

"There's somethin' queer about this sodbuster," the cowhand said.

Hugh Garden gave a weary shrug, as if to say, You just now findin' *that* out? But he hauled on his hackamore and kicked the mule and rode back to see what the trouble was. He rode up in time to see Nash make a grab for the concho. Morrasey quickly jerked it away and rammed it into the pocket of his overalls.

"What's this all about?" Garden demanded.

The young cowhand was beginning to get red in the face. He stared at the sodbuster as though he were seeing him—actually seeing him—for the first time. "A silver doodad," Nash said in a tone that was just beginning to be worried. "Concho. Like the Mex cowhands put on their ridin' rigs."

"What about it?"

"I just seen this sodbuster foolin' with one. I recognized it."

The driver scowled in disbelief. "All the Mex conchos in the world, and you recognize *this* one?"

"It belonged to my boss, the one that I come up the trail with. Name of Hank Barstow.

"On the trail Barstow spent all his free time hammerin' them things out of Mex pesos. Said he was goin' to fix up a bridle for his new wife when he got back. It's got Barstow's personal brand scratched on it, the Double-T." He looked at Morrasey. "Make him show it to you."

In his own sluggish way Morrasey was beginning to understand the direction that Nash's accusation was taking. He began to sense the danger.

"All right," Garden sighed with little patience. "There ain't but one way to settle it. Let's take a look at that silver piece, Morrasey."

Morrasey seemed to shrink into himself. He eyed them suspiciously, pulling his red neck into his collarless shirt like a turkey buzzard watching a coyote. "It's mine. I don't have to show it."

"It's not just the concho," Nash said, his mind slowly closing around the kernel of one harsh, ugly fact. "There's a bone-handle pocketknife that he was cuttin' his fingernails with back at the last station. It hit me at the time;

Hank Barstow had a knife just like that."

"They's lots of bone-handle pocketknives!" Morrasey objected.

"That one belonged to Hank Barstow."

"Look here," Morrasey shouted indignantly at the driver, "I don't have to set here and listen to no cowhand that ain't hardly weaned off his ma's milk yet!"

The driver held out his hand. "Let's take a look at that concho."

"I don't have to! I'm the same's anybody else, ain't I? I paid my way on your mud wagon like the others."

"That's another thing," the young cowhand said, his voice growing quieter and colder. "How many squatter sodbusters do you know, driver, that's got money to ride stagecoaches all the way from No Man's Land to the Colorado?"

Morrasey pulled his head in between his bony shoulders and looked more buzzardlike than ever. "I'm good as anybody! I don't have to listen to this!"

Hugh Garden's look of patient boredom had gradually drained from his face. He regarded the sodbuster with hard, unblinking eyes. "Where *did* you get the money, Morrasey?"

Morrasey's mind was a turmoil. He couldn't think straight. But he could sense the danger that was creeping up on him, silently, unseen, like Kiowa trackers. His only completely formed thought was of the money. It was his, and he wouldn't let them take it from him. No matter what.

"Where did you get the money?" the driver asked again.

The words fell in Morrasey's mind like stones in a turgid pool. The first ripples became waves of panic. How could he convince them that the money was actually his? That cowman would have died *any*way.

". . . Money belt," the young cowhand was saying. "Hank Barstow always wore one. He must of had two hundred dollars with him when he started back to Texas. Morrasey . . ." Morrasey was enraged by the sarcasm that the cowhand put into the word. "Morrasey, are you wearin' a money belt on the underside of them overalls?"

In the cowhand's face Morrasey saw all the things he had ever despised and hated. In a cold, still fury, Ernie Nash was cursing him. "Haul him off that mule," he said to Garden. "See if he ain't wearin' Hank Barstow's money belt."

Garden and Nash closed in on him from opposite sides. With a fire in his brain, Morrasey sat like stone. They were going to rob him. That was the only thought in his mind. They were going to rob him! Without willing it in any way, he threw himself off his mule and began clawing at the startled cowhand.

His bony hands fastened like hawk's talons around Nash's throat and pulled him out of the saddle. Morrasey was dimly aware of Garden's shouting, and of rolling in the dirt, and of savagely banging the young cowhand's head on the rutted clay of the stage road. He saw Nash struggling to free his .45 from its holster. Then they were both fighting for the gun and there was an explosion. A strangely muffled explosion. The muzzle of the .45 had been turned into the cowhand's groin when it went off.

Morrasey threw the suddenly limp figure away from him and fell back panting. He watched without much interest as Hugh Garden threw himself off the mule and stared at

Morrasey with fear and loathing. Then the driver began to curse. He drew his ancient .44, pointed it directly at Morrasey, and pulled the trigger.

The weapon missed fire—not an unusual occurrence with old cap and ball revolvers converted for the use of metal cartridges. Morrasey heard the hammer fall, and that was when he discovered that he had the cowhand's .45 in his hand. He cocked it as if he had all the time in the world. He pointed it at the driver and calmly pulled the trigger.

The result was amazing. The driver was thrown back two steps, whirled half around, and slammed to the ground. His chest was incredibly bloody. Morrasey had never imagined that killing a man could be such an easy and simple matter. This was the first time in his life that he had ever had a revolver in his hands. And two men were dead.

He looked at the two bodies, wondering bleakly what to do with them. He had no tool to dig with, so burying was out of the question. Still, he knew that sooner or later the men would be missed, and some sort of search party would probably be sent out from Bosen's Grove. Without bothering to work it out in his mind, Morrasey sensed that nobody would believe his story of attempted robbery—nobody ever believed a sodbuster about anything.

What I've got to do, he thought calmly, is drag the driver and that cowhand away from the road. Cover them up with brush, rocks, something like that. Sooner or later the buzzards or coyotes would nose them out, but not right away.

Morrasey went about his task in a workmanlike manner. He dragged the two bodies behind a sand knoll, perhaps a hundred yards from the stage road. For almost an hour he gathered rocks and bits of brush and thistles and covered the bodies. Then he stood back at a distance and critically regarded his handiwork.

It wasn't a bad job, he had to admit, with a little ripple of pride. If it wasn't for varmints, the bodies of the cowhand and the driver might remain undiscovered for a year or more.

Not until he was fully satisfied with his handling of the bodies did Morrasey turn his thoughts to what he would do next. He hunkered on a sand knoll, took a bite of tobacco, and considered. First thing he had to do was get back to his place and see about Delly. That was the *first* thing. Then he had to get Delly and himself out of these parts. Clear out of Texas. No sense even wondering what would happen to him if the law got him. He had lived long enough to know how cow-country juries dealt with squatters. Squatters that killed cowmen—such a thing would not even bear thinking about.

For it was now a clear fact—and not even Morrasey could escape it—that he had killed a cowman. No matter that it was an accident. The young cowhand was dead and Morrasey had killed him. To lose sight of that fact would be fatal.

It wasn't until this moment that Morrasey discovered that the mules were gone. The noise of the scuffle and the shooting had spooked them and they had bolted.

It didn't seem possible that three animals as large as mules could have disappeared in country that appeared to be perfectly flat. But the country was not as flat as it appeared. It was pitted with old buffalo wallows, scarred with gullies and dry washes and cut banks. The mules might be in any one of them.

Morrasey shrugged his bony shoulders and took it philosophically. He had walked all the way from the Colorado to Kansas; no reason why he couldn't walk a little farther.

For the three remaining passengers it had been a long, hot day, and the night didn't promise to be much better. "Seems like somebody ought to of been here by this time," Callahan was saying for what was the fourth or fifth time.

Owen Tragg looked up at the startling array of stars and judged it to be almost midnight. "Still a little early, most likely. The driver wouldn't get to Bosen's Grove much before sundown. Then the stage agent would have to get together a rig of some kind to come after us."

Callahan cursed and lit one of his stubby cigars. "They ought to know we're caught here with no grub and damn little water. And no animals. We ought to of kept one of the mules here, just in case."

The same thought had occurred to Tragg, but no use worrying about it now. He walked off a little way from the wrecked mud wagon. There was something about Callahan that rubbed him the wrong way, and he found it almost impossible to talk to the man for five minutes without running a temper.

Jessie Ross was bedded down near the mud wagon, but Tragg and Callahan had preferred to put off sleeping until they got to Bosen's Grove.

"Tragg . . ."

Tragg turned and saw that Jessie was now sitting against the rear wheel of the mud wagon doing something to her hair. He moved toward her and said, "Might be a good notion to get some sleep, Miss Ross."

"I'm not as sleepy as I thought, I guess." She hesitated. "Are you beginnin' to get a funny feeling?"

"About what?"

"About the three men that pulled out with our mules this mornin'. About the stage company that hasn't sent any-body to fetch us."

"There hasn't been time enough for that."

She looked at him quietly. She had taken her hair down and was methodically brushing it. "You sure about that, Marshal?"

"I'm not a marshal," he said automatically. He kept saying that and people kept calling him Marshal. It gave him the uneasy feeling that the person inside this out-landish rig was not Owen Tragg at all but an imitation man created especially for the stage and lecture platform.

Jessie Ross shrugged off his disclaimer. "I still think we ought to of seen somebody from the stage company by this time. Is there any more water?"

Tragg got the driver's canteen for her. She poured a little of the warm water in her hands and patted it on her face. "I feel dried out and old," she said. "Like my ma must of felt before she died."

Tragg could think of nothing to say to that. He was aware of Callahan watching them with a crooked grin of amusement. "Coly," she said wistfully to herself, "used to tell me how pretty I was."

"Coly?"

Her face was in deep shadow and Tragg could not see her expression, but he could sense the way she froze. "Somebody I used to know," she said after a brief silence.

"Coly Brown?"

There was another silence, a taut one this time. "What makes you say that?"

"The only Coly I know with a price on his head," Tragg said brutally. He capped the canteen and put it away. Then he walked away from the mud wagon.

Callahan came after him. "Now you know," he said coldly. "I might of knowed it wouldn't be long. Leave it to a woman to tell everything that's in her head." He hurled his smoldering cigar to the ground. "I hope you're not gettin' any fancy notions, Marshal."

"About what?"

"About the bounty on Coly Brown. Me and the Ross woman's got an understandin' about that. Half for me and half for her, when she turns Coly in. If you get anything out of it, it'll have to be from her." He cocked his head, looking threateningly at Tragg. Then, suddenly and unexpectedly, he laughed. "It couldn't be that Marshal Owen Tragg aims to go after Coly himself, could it? Might not be a bad notion at that. Coly'd take one look at that outfit of yours and fall down in a fit of laughin'. You could take him without no trouble at all."

Callahan was grinning widely in admiration of his own humor. In moonlight, Tragg's face looked deathly pale.

"You might as well put it out of your mind, Marshal," Callahan chuckled. "Coly's a long ways from here, and nobody but Coly's woman knows just where."

Tragg stood very still and erect, taking a professional measure of Callahan. Ten years ago Callahan would not have dared to speak like this to Owen Tragg. But then, ten years ago Tragg had been a real lawman. He said stiffly,

"I'm not interested in Coly or the bounty."

"How about Coly's woman?" Callahan grinned. "Seems like every time I look, she's jawin' with you."

A little of the old Owen Tragg came to the surface. He pulled his head back and gazed levelly at Callahan. "If it's all the same with everybody," he said quietly, "I'd just as soon not get a fuss started. Not before we get to Bosen's Grove, anyway. But if you just won't have it . . ."

Callahan looked mildly surprised. "No call for takin' that tone, Marshal. I was just talkin'."

Tragg was glad enough to let the matter drop. He walked back to the mud wagon, threw a blanket beside the broken wheel, and bleakly wondered what he was going to say to Rose Barker when he saw her.

Somehow the night had worn itself out. Tragg roused himself out of an uneasy sleep. Jessie Ross was shaking his shoulder and saying, "There's still nobody from the stage company. You can't say now that they haven't had time."

The steely light of early dawn lay on the prairie. The eastern horizon glowed like the edge of a bloody sword. Tragg felt chilled to the bone. "Where's Callahan?"

"He threw his blanket over there." She nodded toward the other side of the wagon. "What do you think?"

"I don't know . . ." His mouth felt gritty. He would have given half of everything he owned—which came to about twenty dollars and a stage ticket to El Paso—for a cup of strong coffee.

Callahan came around the rear of the mud wagon shaking the canteen. "Goin' to be a long day, with no grub and just about a quart of water." He looked at Jessie Ross and said with mock gallantry, "Do we wait here, or do we strike for Bosen's Grove on foot?" Clearly, the last thing Callahan intended was separating himself from Coly Brown's woman.

Jessie looked at Tragg. "How far is it?"

"Thirty miles. Maybe a little more. Farther'n I'd care to walk in one day, under this sun." Suddenly he got to his feet, gazing out at the lightening horizon. Callahan and Jessie saw it almost immediately, the ironlike figure in the distance, back-lighted by the hard morning sky. It was the stage mule that young Ernie Nash had ridden away on almost twenty-four hours ago; it was still wearing the cowhand's cherished saddle.

Callahan grunted his surprise. "What the hell!" He started toward the mule, but the animal shied suspiciously and suddenly bolted toward a mesquite thicket. Within a matter of seconds the mule had disappeared behind a knoll. Callahan jogged on for a short distance and then pulled up. "No use," he puffed. "If that mule don't want to be caught, he won't be caught. What do you make of it, Marshal?" For once he managed the word "marshal" without a sneer in his voice.

Owen Tragg shook his head. "Something's happened to that young cowhand. He'd as soon lose his ropin' arm as his saddle."

"What about the mud-wagon driver and the sodbuster? It don't make much sense that they would set still and let the cowhand lose his mule? Unless," he added with a scowl, "somethin' happened to *them.*"

"What could of happened to them here in the middle of

the prairie?" Jessie Ross wanted to know.

Callahan shrugged. Jessie looked worriedly at Tragg, and the former lawman said, "Maybe there's a way station somewhere between here and Bosen's Grove. Might be a good idea to start walkin' that way, just in case."

"Well . . ." She didn't like the prospect of crossing this wasteland on foot, but the alternative of remaining with the wrecked mud wagon seemed less inviting. "How're we goin' to carry our grips?"

"We'll have to leave them. The stage company will send somebody after them later."

Callahan had strolled off a way and was idly smoking a stub of a cigar. He had no plans of his own, except to make sure that he didn't lose sight of Jessie Ross. Wherever she went, he would go. Until he had his part of the bounty, anyway. He watched with mild curiosity as Tragg got his valise out of the boot and opened it. He stood for a time in frowning indecision before taking anything from it.

It was the custom for most men, even drummers, to go armed when traveling. Callahan had found it curious that a man of Tragg's history had thus far displayed no weapon of any kind. Tragg hesitated for perhaps a full minute, gazing bleakly into his opened valise. At last he took out a cartridge belt and a worn leather holster. He slung the belt around his middle and buckled it. Then he took out an unmistakable parcel carefully wrapped in oiled rags, and a subtle but instant change occurred in the appearance and bearing of the man called Owen Tragg.

Tragg himself was aware of the change. He was now a man with a gun, something that he had sworn he would never be again. But vows and ideals had to give way to common sense. This was wild country, and with Callahan, he had the responsibility of seeing a woman safely to Bosen's Grove. Or at least to a way station.

Slowly, he unwrapped the plain wood-handled .45 and checked it. He cleaned five cartridges with the oily rag and thumbed them into the cylinder, easing the hammer down on the empty chamber. He dropped the revolver into the holster.

After ten years of not wearing a gun it was surprising how heavy a single-action Colt could be. He closed the valise and put it back into the boot. Without further discussion, Tragg and Callahan, with the woman between them, began walking into the summer sun.

Jessie Ross was the first to notice the spiraling dark wings against the dazzling sky. Warily, the raw-necked scavengers rose from what appeared to be a rocky knoll. Tragg and Callahan watched them for a moment, and then Callahan said, "Wouldn't hurt anything to look."

Tragg waited with Jessie beside the stage road. They had been walking half a day and the only living things they had seen were a few head of longhorn cattle, wild as deer, and dangerous as cougars to anyone foolish enough to go near them unmounted.

A dark shadow slid across the rocky flatland, almost touching Tragg and the woman. Jessie shuddered. "I hate redneck buzzards almost as much as anything I can think of!"

"They can't hurt you. Most likely they just spotted a dead calf."

But Tragg didn't believe it. Something in his bones told him that what Callahan would find on that knoll would be no calf.

Callahan topped the knoll and disappeared for a while on the other side. When he appeared again and came toward them, Tragg noted the downturned lines around the big man's mouth. "Well," he said dryly, lighting another of his stubby cigars, "now we know what happened to the cow-hand and the stage driver."

Jessie made a thin little sound and stared in fascination as Callahan got his cigar burning just right. After a moment Tragg asked, "What about Morrasey?"

"That sodbuster?" Callahan laughed without humor. "The cowhand and the driver was shot right through the gizzard. Point-blank, from the looks of things. Their pockets turned wrong side out, nothin' on them. Not even their tobacco. You can make up your own mind about Morrasey."

Jessie Ross stared wide-eyed from one man to the other. Suddenly she wheeled and stared fearfully at the waste-land of rocks and brush. Callahan grinned. "No use lookin' for Morrasey out there. Must be at least twenty-four hours since he did the killin'—most likely he's took hisself just as far away as that mud-wagon mule can carry him."

"Didn't he say he had a place not far from Bosen's Grove?" Tragg asked. "A farm of some kind."

Callahan shrugged. He didn't really care about Mor-rasey, or the dead men, or anything else. Only Jessie Ross and the bounty that she was to collect.

Jessie turned and gazed back at the twisting length of wagon track. "Don't anybody ever travel this road, except the mud wagon?"

Neither Callahan nor Tragg bothered to answer. It was

not likely that many wagons would be traveling to Bosen's Grove from the north. Visiting cowhands would find it more convenient to ride cross-country. Tragg said, "There's not much we can do without diggin' tools. Except pile some rocks on the bodies."

"What good would it do?" Callahan asked without interest.

"It would keep the coyotes away for a little while." Tragg glanced at Jessie Ross. "Better get a little rest. This won't take long."

Callahan lounged beside the road smoking, watching Tragg gather up the larger rocks and pile them around the bodies. At last he turned and looked at the woman. His voice was surprisingly cold with deep-running anger. "You just had to go and tell that medicine show marshal about the bounty, didn't you?"

She flushed and started to reply with heat of her own. "That's none of your business!"

"I told you before. Anything you do about the bounty on Coly Brown is my business." He took himself in hand and made his tone quieter, less threatening. "Not that it makes any difference. There was a time, I guess, when Owen Tragg was a good enough lawman. He ain't much now. See the way he handled that .45 when he took it out of his grip today? Like it was a sheddin' copperhead. Sure sign of a man that's lost his nerve."

He sighed and suddenly snapped his burnt-out cigar into a cluster of weeds. "If you've been schemin' to get Tragg to help you, forget it. He may be gettin' old, but he don't strike me as no fool." He grinned and added brutally, "Maybe there was a time, when you caught Coly, that you wasn't a hard-lookin' woman. But right now you ain't no bargain. So if it's crossed your mind that maybe you could sweet-talk that tasseled marshal into killin' me so's you can keep all the bounty for yourself—you might as well put that notion right out of your mind, ma'am."

When Tragg returned from his task he was quick to sense the wall of hostility that had grown up between Callahan and the woman. He could guess that it had something to do with the bounty, but he was not interested. In another day or so, after he had finished his business in Bosen's Grove, he would be moving on and would probably never see them again. Except for that one time, he had never accepted scalp money, and he had no intention of accepting any on Coly Brown.

"Nothin' much we can do about Morrasey," he said, more to himself than to the others. "There must be a law of some kind in Bosen's Grove; he'll know what to do about it."

"If we ever get to Bosen's Grove," Jessie Ross said wearily.

They walked on through the blazing afternoon. They finished the water well before sundown and threw the canteen away. Then, like a dusty green line drawn across the prairie, they saw the scattered salt cedars. Callahan stared at them and rubbed his cracked lips. "Must be a creek! I just hope them salt cedars ain't sapped it dry!"

What once must have been a river was now only a trickle, and that hot and tasting of alkaline, but welcome all the same. They drank sparingly but washed their faces and reveled in the feel of water on their skins. At last they rested in the shade of the twisting cedars, staring dumbly up at the westering sun.

"How far to Bosen's Grove?" Jessie Ross asked finally.

No one answered. It was too far to comfortably think about. Another day's walk, at the rate they were going. Jessie's spool-heeled shoes and Tragg's thin-soled riding boots were already in poor condition.

After a time Callahan climbed the opposite bank and stood for several minutes, trying to discover some sign of life in that wasteland. Jessie looked at Tragg and asked, for apparently no reason at all, "What do you aim to do when you get to El Paso?"

The question caught him by surprise. "I'm not sure," he said slowly. "Find a job, I guess. Go to work."

"You goin' back to lecturin'?"

He smiled faintly. "No. I'm through with that."

"Back to bein' a lawman then?"

"Maybe," he said, after some hesitation. "There's somebody I used to know that's in with the county sheriff. Thinks he can get me on there, or with the police."

"A man with your reputation . . ." She sounded genuinely puzzled. "It ought to be easy."

Tragg looked to see if she was serious. "Ten years is a long time," he told her. "Not many folks wants a platform lecturer for a lawman."

"Them the only things you know? Lawin' and lecturin'?"

Another of those heatless smiles touched the corners of his mouth. "Just about." Lawin' and lecturin'. Through with one and afraid of the other.

"Well," she pressed, as though she were actually interested, "what do you aim to do?"

64

It was a legitimate question. One that he would sooner or later have to answer himself. It had been over a year since Webb Faver had promised to get him a place in the sheriff's office. Maybe Webb was not even there himself by this time. All this time he had been holding to that hope that Webb could get him a desk job. There was a lot of paperwork in a sheriff's office—Tragg was familiar with the work and knew that he could do it. But if they sent him out as a regular deputy, with a badge and a gun—

His answer to Jessie Ross was a faint half smile and shrug.

Then, with a suddenness that startled him, she asked, "Why are you layin' over in Bosen's Grove?"

For a moment it seemed that Tragg had turned to stone. He looked down at her, and in his face there was no smile or hint of a smile. It was a look that spoke far more precisely than words. You ask too many questions, young woman. Entirely too many questions.

She was surprised at his reaction but refused to be put off by it. "You know this country pretty good," she said easily, as though nothing had happened.

". . . I used to."

"You happen to know an old Mex by the name of Valona?"

Tragg frowned. "Don Carlos Valona? Big sheepman from the other side of the Cap Rock. Sheepmen don't usually range this far east."

She studied him quietly for several seconds. From the sleeve of her dress she drew out a tattered broadside and handed it to him.

Tragg understood immediately. The message was brief

65

and to the point. $10,000 REWARD FOR INFORMA-
TION CONCERNING THE WHEREABOUTS OF
COLY (COLBY) BROWN WHO ON THE 15th DAY OF
AUGUST, 1887, NEAR BOSEN'S GROVE, TEXAS,
ROBBED THE MILO BROS. EXPRESS COACH,
KILLING THE DRIVER AND ONE PASSENGER.
Signed: Carlos CoroVega y Valona.

It was not the regular sort of poster that circulated
among the county and local law-enforcement officers. It
was privately printed on good paper and had been
signed by what was presumably Don Carlos' own hand.
The message made no mention of arrest or conviction—
only information concerning the whereabouts of Coly
Brown.

Tragg returned the broadside and asked dryly, "You
think it's goin' to be as simple as that? Just walk up to old
Don Carlos and tell him where Coly's hidin' and collect
your money?"

"I don't see why not."

"You know what'll happen, don't you, when Valona
finds him?"

She shrugged, but she did not look at Tragg's eyes.

"If it happens to be Coly's lucky day," Tragg went on in
the same emotionless tone, "Valona's pistoleros might be
satisfied with shooting him to death on the spot. If he
doesn't happen to be lucky they'll probably crucify him to
the ground, looking at the sun."

Her eyes widened. Involuntarily, she shuddered. But she
carefully took the broadside, folded it, and slipped it back
in her sleeve for safekeeping. "You're lyin'. Nobody

would do a thing like that!"

It was nothing to Tragg. After a while the three of them started walking again, following the wagon track south.

CHAPTER FIVE

ORRASEY sat on a rock to get his breath and to empty some gravel out of his battered shoes. Lord, he thought, looking out at the parched landscape, what a poor country this is! Off to the west he could see the familiar green swath that marked the banks of Dead Man's Creek. There were a lot of Dead Man's Creeks in this part of Texas—there was hardly a stream anywhere that hadn't been fought over at one time or another. Sometimes it seemed that water, in this land, was more precious than blood.

Off to the west of this particular Dead Man's Creek was Morrasey's place. He could see it in his mind—the sod hut, the sterile slope on which he had known nothing but failure. In the beginning he had thought to cultivate a place in the creek bottom, but that futile dream had been killed at once by the cowman who owned the headwater. So Morrasey and Delly had to move on, taking whatever they could find.

Well, Morrasey promised himself, from now on things would be different. No longer would he stand for being pushed this way and that, on the say-so of cowmen. He sat for several minutes with the sun beating down on him, rubbing his calloused feet, thinking of Delly and the better times that were to come. Just you wait! he thought, with the thump of excitement in his chest. Just you wait, Delly, until you see what I brought you!

Suddenly he was taken by a sense of urgency. He pulled on his frayed brogans and lurched to his feet, and for perhaps a full minute he stood listening with painful concentration, listening to the humming silence of that malignant wasteland. Won't be long now, he told himself. You just hold on, Delly. I'll be there before you know it.

He started toward that stroke of green on the brown prairie, walking fast, almost running. In a fit of impatience he flung away the tow-sack grip that he had carried all the way to Kansas and back. A few rags was all that was in it. He didn't need it. He had money now.

By the time he reached Dead Man's Creek he was gasping for air and his heart felt as if it were trying to tear itself out of his chest. He fell down beside the stream and drank his fill and threw some water on his head. Then he lay quietly until his legs stopped quivering. He didn't know what had got into him, racing across the prairie like a cow on locoweed. But he couldn't rest, even now, and as soon as his legs would support him he pushed himself to his feet and stumbled on.

Several times within the next hour he had to stop and rest. He found the unaccustomed weight of the cowhand's .45 irritating and tiring, and once he unbuckled it and threw it away. But after a moment he went back for it and buckled it on again. That weapon had come in mighty handy once. The time might come when he would need it again.

He stumbled on, unmindful now of the heat and his own exhaustion, driven on by that sense of urgency that he could not explain.

For a moment, when he first caught sight of the place, he pulled himself up and stared at it and breathed a little easier. It looked just the same as it always had. The sod hut, the brush arbor, the red chickens scratching in what passed as a dooryard. Delly was nowhere in sight, but at first he thought nothing of that. She was probably busy inside the hut. Then he realized that the work mule was missing from the rawhide corral beside the brush arbor, and the gate was down. There was no sign of Delly or the mule in the patch of brown cotton stubbles below the hut.

Something inside Morrasey shriveled and died. Although the sun was scorching hot, he folded his bony arms across his chest and shivered. The sense of urgency mysteriously left him, and in its place there was only an aching void in his guts and the insane notion that he was freezing.

His mind was remarkably still and empty as he started down the slight grade toward the hut. His legs seemed to move of their own accord. He was painfully aware of the prairie's humming silence.

As he drew nearer he saw that the brush arbor was leaning crazily with the south wind. It needed to be braced every week or so, and he could see that this had not been attended to. This small fact lay like a lead bullet in the bottom of his mind.

Morrasey pulled up beside a thornbush in the dooryard. "Delly! I'm back! Come see what I brought you!"

One of the chickens cocked its head and clucked at him. He started toward the hut, walking fast. Then he broke into a run.

"Delly!"

The hut was empty. It had that dry, shucked-off feeling of a place that had not been lived in for a long time. Morrasey stared at the dirt walls and at the dirt roof. Where had she gone?

He ducked through the doorway and shouted at the top of his voice, "Delly, where are you!"

Those vast spaces devoured sound so quickly and so thoroughly that he was not quite sure whether he had actually shouted or if he had only imagined it.

He tried to think where she might have gone. Not to a neighbor's. They had no neighbors. Only a line camp, a mile or so to the east, that belonged to one of the local cowmen.

From some secret chamber tucked far away in some dark corner of his mind, a still voice said, "You know where she's gone to. You know." But Morrasey did not listen. Maybe, he told himself, she went looking for poke greens.

Poke greens in the heat of summer? In a land so barren that even mesquite and cactus had to scratch for survival?

He walked over to the brush arbor and said in a quiet conversational tone, "Delly?"

He walked on down to the dry wash behind the hut and stood for some time gazing down at the sandy bottom. Once every year or so it ran bankfull for a day or two, when the spring floods came, and for the rest of the time it was dry. Morrasey had built his hut here in the foolish hope that someday, somehow, this dry wash would miraculously become a fresh flowing stream. Of course, he thought now, it wouldn't really make any difference if the miracle did happen. The cowmen would soon figure out a way to do him out of it.

"Delly?"

He climbed down the bank of baked red clay and walked along the sandy bottom. From time to time he would stop and look around and ask, "Delly?" Then he would move on.

At last he left the wash and tramped heavily along the rocky knolls overlooking the hut. He found himself remembering snatches of fiddle tunes. The happy times. Laughter. The wailing of fiddles and the good-natured stomping of country dancers. And Delly, as light on her feet as a young doe deer. The prettiest girl he'd ever seen.

"Delly?"

Morrasey was sitting on the ground in back of the hut when he saw the horsebacker. He had been there a long while. Not thinking, not doing anything, just sitting. He saw that it was early morning and that he was damp with dew.

The horsebacker, an old-timer that Morrasey dimly recognized as one of the line riders from the nearby camp, reined toward the sodbuster, cautiously noting the glazed look of the man's eyes and his deathlike listlessness. He brought his dun to a halt, looked down at Morrasey, and nodded. "Thought I seen somebody down here, but I wasn't sure." He indicated the hut and the arbor with another nod. "This place belong to you?"

Morrasey looked at him for several seconds. At last he nodded.

The rider shifted and looked ill at ease. "Name's Billy Sewell. Me and my pard batch up at the line shack, north of here." Morrasey gave no indication that he had heard. "We ride line for Mr. Jessup," the cowhand added hopefully.

Morrasey dwelled for a moment on the name of Omar

Jessup. He had reason enough to know and hate that name. It had been Jessup's hands who had chivied Morrasey and Delly until they had had to leave the bottom land. "What do you want?"

Billy Sewell's gaze became curiously unfocused. "Tell you the truth, mister . . ." He didn't even know the sodbuster's name. "Tell you the truth, I'm scared I've got hard news for you."

"What about?" Morrasey was thinking about a time, long ago. One of the agent's girls from the Cherokee country had married a soldier from Reno, and there was a party that lasted almost four days. Morrasey and Delly hadn't missed a minute of it. That was the way it had been in those days, the good days. Travel clear across Kansas and half of Indian Territory to attend a play party or a fiddling.

"Well," Billy Sewell said, sweating freely, "it's about your wife. I sure never wanted to be the one to have to tell you, but I guess there ain't anybody else."

Morrasey was still back in the Cherokee Hills. Folks had come all the way from Red River, just for that party. Outlawed whisky by the kegful. A whole beef roasting over a fire pit. Two brothers from Fort Smith that claimed to be the best fiddlers in Arkansas. Morrasey tried to recall the name of those brothers, but for the moment it eluded him.

The cowhand leaned forward in the saddle, his eyes sad and concerned, "Mister," he asked quietly, "did you hear me? I said it was about your wife. Me and my pard—that's Slim Hardy—we done the best we could. We buried her over there in the cleared-off place, on the other side of the cotton."

Like water soaking into a cheap felt hat, the cowhand's

words soaked into Morrasey's mind. The evil sense of the words became clear. "You buried her." Saying the words was like drinking poison more bitter than gall.

Making no attempt to get to his feet, Morrasey stared up at the cowhand and realized that he was an old man. His stubble of beard was almost white, his face was sun-cured to the color of old Spanish leather. Abiding by the cherished rule of southwest hospitality, Sewell had remained in the saddle, waiting for Morrasey's invitation to dismount. Then he realized that expecting hospitality, or even decent manners, from a sodbuster was too much to ask. Slowly, he climbed down and took a few steps toward Morrasey, holding to the reins.

"It was my pard, Slim Hardy, that found her," the old-timer said with compassion. Just because the man was a sodbuster didn't mean he didn't have feelings, although many of Billy's friends would have been quick to argue the matter. With a kind of dying wildness in his eyes, Morrasey stared at him. Billy rushed on, eager to get it over with.

"This was—let me see—six, seven days ago. Slim and me was ridin' together, and Slim says, 'There's somethin' down there by the sodbuster's place. Looks like a downed calf.' But it wasn't no calf. We saw that, when we rode a little closer. Well . . ." He seemed to shrink a little and did not look directly into Morrasey's eyes. "Well, what it was was a woman. Your wife. She was finished. There wasn't nothin' we could do for her. Best we could figger, she'd been dead two, three days. No tracks around. No sign of a scuffle. Looked like she just walked off from the house and set down on a rock, and kept settin' there until she died."

The cowhand sensed that he was telling it badly, but he

knew of no other way to go about it. "We scouted the place," he continued, "for maybe an hour, lookin' for some sign of life. There wasn't any. Just the chickens. Me and Slim got to talkin' and wonderin' where the man was, and we figgered he must of struck out by hisself to look for work. This bein' a hard year for farmin'. Hard on cowmen, too, far as that goes."

Morrasey stared but did not try to speak or move. Billy Sewell had the disquieting feeling that he was doing all this talking and explaining to the open prairie. There was no way of knowing if the sodbuster had understood a word of what he was saying. Well, Billy told himself, this wouldn't be the first sodbuster that went a little loco during a hard year. And he guessed the woman wouldn't be the first to become so despaired that she simply sat down and died. This was the kind of country where such things happened.

"Didn't seem like there was anything else to do," the cowhand said, speaking faster, now that he was almost finished. "Slim found a shovel over there under the arbor, and we took turns diggin'. That's mighty hard ground, I can tell you. I ain't surprised that your cotton failed. But we stayed at it and done you a good job, even if I do say so myself. Smoothed the sides, made the corners nice and square. I looked around, but there wasn't any lumber to make a box out of. We wrapped her in a piece of white muslin. Sheet, I guess it was. We found it there in the house. . . ."

Morrasey rose up on his haunches. He howled like an old he-coyote howling at a full moon.

It was a sound that Billy Sewell would not soon forget. Involuntarily he raised a hand as if to ward off a wild beast. But it was doubtful that Morrasey was even aware that he was standing there.

Sheriff Max Ellender stared at Tragg in disbelief. His feverish eyes showed his revulsion as he minutely studied every tasseled and beaded and conchoed item of Tragg's outlandish dress. "What in God's name," he asked wearily, "are you got up for?"

Tragg felt himself coloring. He wished now that he had bought some suitable clothing when he was in Dodge. He started to explain about the ten-year lecture tour that had finally ground to a stop in Dodge City, then almost immediately changed his mind. To hell, he thought bitterly, with this obscure county sheriff and whatever his objections may be to tassels and beads.

"Sheriff," he said with decided coolness, "I just got to Bosen's Grove a few minutes ago. Me and two other passengers on the Tascosa stage . . ."

Sheriff Ellender lurched up in bed and cursed savagely at his awkwardly splinted leg. Just two days before he had broken the leg while helping a local cowman load his wagon. After a dozen years of working cattle in the treacherous brush country, he had to break his leg by falling with a fifty-pound sack of coffee. He was in considerable pain and certainly in no mood to pass the time with any fool that would dress himself in a tasseled buckskin hunting shirt.

"We been wonderin' about that mud wagon," he snarled, as though all his pain and inconvenience was the personal work of Owen Tragg. "Hugh Garden's been known to take a drop too much in Tascosa and be maybe a day late gettin' here. Still . . ." He was a lean, hard-eyed man in his middle years, struggling vainly for some kind of dignity while wearing nothing but slats on his leg and a gray flannel nightshirt.

"The mud wagon broke a wheel," Tragg explained. "And an axle."

Ellender sank back on his sweat-damp pillow and closed his eyes. "Well, that explains it. I keep tellin' the county that they ought to grade that damn wagon track. But who listens to a county sheriff?" He opened one eye and squinted unhappily at Tragg. "Where's the driver now?"

". . . He's dead."

Guiltily, Tragg realized that he had wanted to shock some semblance of decent behavior into this man who was too occupied with pain to concern himself with such things. His effort was at least partially successful. The sheriff stared wide-eyed for perhaps a half a minute before speaking.

"What happened? Did he get throwed off the driver's box?"

"He was shot." Even before the words were spoken, Tragg was ashamed of his part in this childish game. "I'm sorry," he apologized. "We've had a long walk. I guess I'm tired." He managed a small smile. "I'll start at the beginnin' and tell you what I know."

The sheriff listened intently until Tragg was finished. Then he groaned and asked, "Morrasey? You sure that was the sodbuster's name?"

"That's what he said. He boarded the stage up in No Man's Land."

"Guess it was Morrasey, all right. I heard he'd struck north lookin' for work."

"You know him then?"

The sheriff nodded. "Squatter. Not many of them left in this county. Land's too hard for them." He lay for a minute in angry silence. "I'm supposed to have a deputy," he said at last, "but Lord knows where he is now. I sent him south two days ago to look into a robbery complaint—no way of knowin' what he's doin' or when he'll get back. Morrasey could cause this county a mess of trouble if somebody don't stop him."

"Might be I figgered it all wrong," Tragg said. "I just told it the way it looked to me. Could be, I guess, that Morrasey had a reason for doin' what he did."

"He had a reason," Ellender said dully, "but not one that a jury would listen to. Hard times and dry weather. I wonder where he got the money to buy a stage ticket."

Tragg shrugged. The problem was not his. He was sore-footed and sour with exhaustion, and his own trouble hadn't even started yet. He still had Rose Barker to talk to. "Well," he said, "I figgered you'd want to know about the driver and that young cowhand." His chin dipped in an abrupt nod of good-by, and he reached for the door.

"Tragg . . ." The sheriff said the word thoughtfully while gazing doubtfully at Tragg's face. "Owen Tragg . . . There used to be a deputy marshal by that name that rode for the court at Fort Smith. That ain't you, is it?"

Tragg sighed to himself and admitted that he was the one.

"I'll be damned." The sheriff was having difficulty matching Tragg's reputation to all those tassels and beads. "Then you must be the one that killed Jody Barker."

". . . That was a long time ago."

"Close to ten years," Ellender agreed, completely

ignoring the chill in Tragg's voice. "Did you know that Jody's widow lives here?"

". . . Yes."

The sheriff gazed at him with obvious interest. Tragg, angry at himself for allowing the talk to take this hated turn, reached again for the door. And again the sheriff stopped him. "Jody was born and raised not far from Bosen's Grove. I guess you knowed that too." When Tragg said nothing, he went on in a tone of quiet speculation. "Jody Barker was a heller, there's no denyin' that. At the same time, he was kind of a likable fool and had a lot of pals in these parts. I don't know what brought you here, and I guess it ain't any of my business. I'm tellin' you this just so you'll know."

"I'm obliged," Tragg said stiffly.

"Don't get your back up," the sheriff told him. "I knowed Jody myself. Somebody had to kill him, sooner or later. Seemed like that was the thing he was born for." He studied Tragg through slitted eyes. "But if somebody'd asked me," he went on, "I wouldn't of said you was the right man for the job. Jody was a dead shot. Killed four, five men that I know about. Somehow, I can't quite see . . ."

Tragg had sworn to himself that he would not explain himself or his dress to this quarrelsome back-country sheriff. But the words were out almost before he knew it. "I've been back east, lecturin'."

Sheriff Ellender made a small sound of understanding. "I see." He gestured dismissal with one hand. "Thanks for tellin' me about the driver and the cowhand. I'll get somebody to go after the bodies. And Morrasey . . . I guess Morrasey'll keep till my deputy gets back."

Just as Tragg was going out the door, Ellender said, "Favor for favor, like they say, Tragg. You answered my questions, now I'll answer yours."

"I haven't asked any questions."

"You would have, sooner or later. There's a boardin'-house across from the big water trough at the end of the street. If you're lookin' for Rose Barker, that's where you'll find her."

For a county seat, Bosen's Grove wasn't much of a town. One wagon yard with a livery corral and a few camp shacks, a barbershop-bathhouse, the usual general store and saloons, the six-room hotel where Sheriff Max Ellender was imprisoned. And the nameless boarding-house that Ellender had mentioned. There seemed to be no county buildings, except for the inevitable rock calaboose standing grim and solid behind the livery barn. County business, if there was any, was apparently handled by the officeholders in the secrecy of their own homes.

Stage company business was handled by the hotelkeeper who used his personal room as an office. Tragg stopped by on his way from the sheriff's room to see about the next stage to El Paso.

"Just missed her," the hotel man told him cheerfully. "Come in this mornin' from Fort Griffin and pulled right out again. Won't be another one for two days." He stared in fascination at Tragg's rig but allowed himself no comment. "I can put you up, if you aim to lay over."

"Not right now." In that wide stretch of dusty prairie that served Bosen's Grove as a main street, the sun seemed to be beating straight down. Tragg had been walking the whole of one day, most of a night, and now it was noon of day again. It occurred to him that he was hungry as well as tired and thirsty. "Where can I find the closest eatin' house?"

The only eating place in town, it turned out, was the boardinghouse at the end of the street. Unless, as the hotel man pointed out, you happened to be strong on pickled pigs' feet, in which case any one of the three saloons might do.

Jessie Ross was waiting for him on the plank walk in front of the hotel. "Did you talk to the sheriff?"

Tragg nodded. "I talked to him." Callahan was lounging in the doorway of a saloon, watching them.

"Well? What did he say?"

"He's sendin' a rig out to pick up the bodies. The stage agent's sendin' somebody to get our grips."

"That's not what I mean." She fanned the hot air impatiently. "What did he say about the old Mex, Carlos Valona?"

Tragg stared at her. For a moment he had forgotten the mission that had brought her such a great distance at so much expense and discomfort. "Valona's no interest of mine," he said coldly. "If you want to know about him you'll have to do the askin' yourself." He turned on his heel and walked away.

"Where're you goin'?" Jessie asked in alarm. She quickly fell in beside him, almost running to keep up with him.

"I'm goin' to the wagon yard and see if they've got a camp shack where I can put up for a while."

"You're not goin' on to El Paso then?"

"I just missed the coach this morning. There won't be another one for two days."

She made a little sound of relief. "I'll go with you."

"Camp shacks," he told her, "are for men and families. They're not for women by theirselves."

She shot him a look of annoyance. Suddenly she grabbed his sleeve and jerked. Tragg spun around in surprise, but he was not surprised to see that Callahan had come out of the saloon and was following them. "Listen to me!" Jessie Ross hissed under her breath. "I can't start askin' all over the town about the Mex that's puttin' up the bounty on Coly. Everybody'd know what I was after. How long do you think I'd last with that money, even if I collected it? Woman by herself in a strange town. And the only lawman in town in bed with a busted leg!"

His instincts told him to brush her aside and stay away from her. But a curiosity that went back to his days as a lawman wouldn't let the matter die so simply. "What is it between you and Callahan? What kind of hold has he got on you that would make you give him half the bounty?"

She laughed harshly. "He *thinks* I'm goin' to give it to him."

"Are you?"

She sighed and they began walking again. The plank sidewalk ended with the last business house, and they took a dirt path toward the livery barn. "I'm scared," she admitted at last. "If I don't give him half the money, Callahan threatens to tell Coly and his bunch that I'm the one that turned them in."

"What would Coly do if he found out?"

"Coly?" The word had a sad, faraway ring. "Coly wouldn't do anything. He's dyin'. Maybe he's dead by this time. Last I seen of him he was burnin' up with fever.

Bullet in his lungs." She turned toward Tragg and her look sharpened, as if he had just said something to offend her. "You don't think I'd turn him in if he wasn't already good as done for, do you?"

Tragg smiled grimly at this unexpected turn in the ethics of scalp hunting. "I hadn't thought about it one way or another."

"Anyhow," she went on dully, "it ain't Coly I'm scared of. It's his pals. They'd have my hide if they found out."

They pulled up in front of the wide-open doors of the barn. "There's one thing here that bothers me," Tragg said. "Why are you tellin' me this? How do you know I won't try to do you out of the bounty, the same as Callahan?"

"You?" Apparently this possibility had never crossed her mind. "No." She shook her head. "You're not the kind. Anyhow, you're a lawman. Or used to be."

"A lot of killers were lawmen at one time or another. Bill Doolin used to ride for the same court that I did."

"Maybe." She didn't sound interested. "But you're not the kind to go after bounties."

"I took a bounty once." The sound of the words appalled him. Many a long night he had lived with the thought, but never before had he spoken it aloud.

"Jody Barker?"

He nodded.

Jessie Ross studied him for a moment, her level gaze flitting here and there over his face. "You must of had a reason," she said with no undue concern. "For that matter, so have I. Will you talk to the sheriff about that old Mex?"

"No," Tragg said stiffly. He turned abruptly and walked away.

CHAPTER SIX

A LL that day Morrasey wandered blind and deaf with grief over the wasted slope that had been his farm. Always he returned to that mound of raw clay and stared at it with dry, wild eyes, trying to understand that this was Delly, his wife. This was the girl that he had loved and married. This was the happy girl with flying hair.

He could not imagine her as she had been the last time he had seen her, a leathery skeleton, empty-eyed, despairing.

From time to time he would tear himself away and stumble to the hut where he would paw dumbly through the meager belongings that had been his and Delly's. He would stare with blazing hatred at the dirt floor and the dirt walls and the dirt roof. Animals. They had lived like animals. Maybe they could have made a go of farming if they had been allowed to work the richer soil of the creek bottom. But not here. Nobody could make a go of farming in such a barren land as this.

In a pot he found a few beans that had spoiled and then dried into a solid, rocklike mass, and a small piece of pan bread as hard as flint. Abstractedly, without thinking or tasting, he ate them.

In a sudden burst of rage he attacked the sod walls of the hut, hammering on them until both fists were raw and bloody. Then he left the hut and once again walked over every foot of worthless land, cursing every foot of it, cursing God for creating such a hellish place. And finally, inevitably, he returned to the grave and, with fire in his brain and knives in his chest, he stared at it and he stared at it, until at last he knew what he had to do.

Omar Jessup's workday began at six o'clock in the morning. The rancher and his two headquarters hands had been up for more than an hour, and first light was just beginning to show on the eastern prairie. Jessup himself did the morning cooking. Dry salt meat, flapjacks, and black molasses; it would never occur to any of them to have anything else for breakfast. They filled their tin plates by the light of a coal-oil lamp and moved outside to eat. Jessup had never married and probably never would—too set in his ways, he said. He was a good cowman and a fair man to work for.

The men took their plates out to the dogtrot that separated living quarters from the cooking quarters of the shotgun style ranch house. They ate in silence, drank their ink-black coffee, and methodically built cigarettes.

Jessup turned to the oldest hand, Red Gipson. "Red, have we got plenty axle grease?"

Gipson grunted, indicating that they did.

"Better mix up a batch of dope and take it up to north camp. Horn flies givin' them fits."

Red said he would get right on it. "Bob," Jessup said to his foreman, Bob Rayburn, "I want that south fence closed all the way around my water rights. You better take the wagon into Bosen and pick up maybe twenty spools of wire. Take your rifle and shoot any coyotes you see along the way."

Bob winced slightly at the mention of fencing. Postholes and aching muscles and blistered hands was what fencing meant to him. Omar Jessup pushed himself to his feet. "I'll be over at the west camp, if anybody wants me."

"Boss . . ." There was a note of worry in Red's voice as Jessup started toward the corral. "You takin' your rifle this mornin'?"

"I always take it." His tone said that Red's question had rubbed him the wrong way. Jessup was a man who didn't like to be made over—which was one reason why he never married. "Are you still frettin' over that sodbuster?"

"A little, I guess. Billy Sewell said he never liked the looks of him. Horseflesh or men, Billy ain't a bad judge."

"Put it out of your head," the cowman told him sternly. "I don't aim to ride out of my way for no sodbuster."

The two hands looked at one another and shrugged. Jessup was a good boss but even his own hands had to admit he was bullheaded.

However, Omar Jessup wasn't so completely unconcerned as he had seemed to his two hands. Billy Sewell was no fool. If he told you a man was dangerous—even if he was only a sodbuster—it might just pay to listen.

The cowman checked the action on his short-barreled Winchester and saw that the magazine was loaded with clean cartridges before starting the day's work. There, he thought comfortably. Even a sodbuster's got more sense than to start trouble with a saddle rifle.

Morrasey didn't even see the rifle. It wouldn't have made the slightest difference if he had. All he saw was the ruddy, well-fed, self-satisfied face of the cowman.

It was sheer luck that the two should meet so soon. Morrasey had been quite prepared for a long search. And here, just like fate, Jessup was riding right into his hands. Omar

Jessup, the man who had fenced Morrasey away from his precious water. Because of that, the farm had failed. And somehow, because of that, Delly was dead. There was not the faintest doubt in Morrasey's mind about this one intolerable fact; because of Jessup's greed, Delly had died.

Well, he thought, that debt would soon be squared. The score would be settled—as far as it was possible to settle one life against another. A little closer, cowman, Morrasey thought to himself. Ride on just a little closer.

And Jessup's horse, almost as if some giant unseen hand had guided it, veered a little to the right and came directly toward Morrasey.

Morrasey had been sitting on a sandstone outcrop getting his breath when he first heard the horsebacker. If he had been standing, Jessup would have seen him, and that would have ruined everything. But he hadn't been standing. Fate. With utmost care Morrasey slid off the rock and lay on his belly in the brown grass. He hauled the .45 out of the holster and studied it for a moment to make sure that he had everything just right. He was surprised all over again at how heavy the weapon was and how much effort it took just to cock it.

He remembered how violently the revolver had jumped in his hand the last time he had used it. This time he would be prepared for that. And the noise. Because he had been successful against the stage driver and the cowhand he was not making the mistake of thinking he knew everything there was to know about firearms. He realized that he didn't. He also realized that his first experience had been mostly luck. Sodbusters learned early in life not to trust to luck.

He knew that he would have to hold his fire until the distance between them was too insignificant to matter. Only then could he trust himself with a short-barreled weapon like a revolver. Too bad it wasn't a rifle. He knew a little something about rifles. Not much, but at least he had shot rabbits with them, and squirrels.

Now Morrasey lay as still as the outcropping itself. Jessup was quite close; it hardly seemed possible that he did not see Morrasey lying there beside the rock. But the cowman's mind was on other things at the moment. Figgerin' how to rob other farmers of their land, Morrasey thought bitterly.

Now the distance between them was narrowing rapidly. Twenty yards. Fifteen. Ten. Morrasey held the .45 in both hands, watching the cowman over the smooth, dark barrel. He was pleased to note that his hands were not shaking. He was not nervous or afraid. He was not even sweating.

When he finally pulled the trigger, Jessup's horse, a fine-boned claybank gelding, was no more than a yard from the muzzle of the revolver. Even so, the first shot, plowing up at a sharp angle, only nicked the cowman's right shoulder. Startled, the claybank reared, almost unseating its rider.

For an instant the entire scene froze in Morrasey's memory. The expression of disbelief and outrage in Jessup's face. His left hand flung out instinctively as an aid in balance, his right hand grabbing hopelessly for the short saddle rifle. Unhurriedly, Morrasey cocked the revolver again and fired the second time.

The second bullet missed its mark altogether. The frightened claybank bolted suddenly, and this time was successful in unseating Jessup. For the moment the cowman ignored his bloody shoulder, ignored Morrasey and the revolver. He kicked savagely at the stirrups but succeeded in freeing only one foot. He fell heavily, his left foot caught in the near stirrup. Morrasey heard the solid sound and the grunt as the cowman's head struck the sun-hardened earth.

The gelding, now in full gallop, raced almost a hundred yards, dragging its rider, before Jessup finally managed to shake himself free. Immediately Morrasey was on his feet and running, trying to cock the revolver as he ran, almost frantic in the momentary belief that Jessup was getting away.

Instinct for survival prompted Jessup to grasp his rifle as he fell, but he lost it immediately. Then he was flying head over heels across the wasteland of rock and brush. The breath was driven from his lungs. The shock of impact was stunning. His eyes lost their focus, his sense of direction and balance was a shambles. But he did not lose consciousness. To do so, he knew, would have meant death. In that first moment of surprise he had seen that much in Morrasey's eyes.

But in the end it made no difference. By the time the falling and tumbling was over he was in no condition to protect himself. He heard the heavy thudding of sodbuster shoes as Morrasey raced toward him, but he did not actually see his assassin himself. He imagined, for just a moment, that he glimpsed the enormous muzzle of the .45—this time Morrasey did not intend to miss—but that was the last thing, the very last thing, that Omar Jessup was ever aware of.

When it was over Morrasey stood panting, the heavy .45, still smoking, dangling carelessly in his hand. Well, he thought with a bleakness that was just bearable, that's that. And then he waited for something to happen. He wasn't sure what he expected, but for the past several hours, which had seemed like an eternity, the point to his whole existence, and the hope of rest for Delly, had been centered in the act of killing Omar Jessup.

But nothing changed. Jessup was dead, but so was Delly. And then, slowly but with a fearful thoroughness, it came to him. It was never going to change. No matter what he did, *it was never going to change.*

Rose Barker was not at all the kind of woman Tragg had expected. Jody Barker had carried a small tintype of his wife at the time of his death, and the image on that small metallic square had haunted Tragg for almost ten years. It was hard to believe that the picture in Tragg's memory could once have been a fair likeness of the woman he now confronted.

The Rose Barker in Tragg's mind was just seventeen years old. A traveling photographer had made the picture the same week she had married Jody. It was a lineless, pretty face of youth, with quiet eyes and soft hair. Tragg had known that she had come from a squatter family and that her childhood had been anything but easy, but that hadn't shown in the picture. She was smiling. She looked happy, the way a young bride ought to look.

The woman staring at him now looked as if she had never smiled.

"Mrs. Barker?" Tragg asked doubtfully. He had found her in the boardinghouse kitchen. Against the far wall a large hay-burning stove assaulted them with waves of heat. The room was even more stifling than Sheriff Ellender's hotel room.

Rose Barker, Tragg knew, could not be much more than twenty-seven. This woman could have passed for twice that age. The many lines about her mouth were deep and hard. Her eyes were faded and spiritless. Apparently she could not bring herself to speak, except to snarl. "What do you want?" she asked, slopping a pot of boiling cabbage to the back of the stove.

Tragg took a deep breath. "My name's Owen Tragg."

Her expression did not change greatly. She turned and regarded him briefly with bitterness and hatred that were so deeply felt that they appeared perfectly natural. She studied his clothing without interest or surprise.

"My job as a lecturer played out a few days ago, up at Dodge. I'm afraid I won't be able to send you anything for a while, but after I'm settled in El Paso . . ."

"I never asked you for anything." Only by the roughness of her voice could he guess the depth of her hatred for him.

"I know," he said.

She seemed to feel that he was reading something in her face, and she turned quickly to the stove. "Get away. I don't want to look at you."

Tragg sighed to himself. The meeting was promising to be even a greater disaster than he had feared. I never should have come here, he thought. What I have to say to her, I could have said in a letter. What did I expect? Forgiveness? From the man who killed her husband? He said wearily, "I just didn't want you to worry when the money stopped for a few weeks. I wanted you to know I'll soon be settled in another job."

"Get away!"

Tragg fell back a step, as if he had been slapped. "Sorry I bothered you, ma'am." He fled the sweltering kitchen as if ghosts had been at his heels. And perhaps they were.

He almost ran into Jessie Ross. She had been standing in the archway that separated the boardinghouse dining room from the kitchen, and it was obvious from her expression that she had overheard most of the strange conversation with Rose Barker.

Tragg pushed past her and seated himself at the plank table. Jessie, who had already eaten, went out to the boardinghouse's front porch to wait. Tragg was suddenly anything but hungry; the overpowering smell of cabbage and grease put his stomach in a knot. A man who appeared to be a storekeeper pushed bowls of cabbage and beans and corn bread toward his end of the table.

Tragg made himself smile. "Much oblige." He dished some of the food onto his plate.

The first rush of dinner business seemed to be over; there were three other men besides Tragg at that long table in the bare room. They ate steadily and silently, with only an occasional curious glance at the newcomer. Tragg put some of the greasy food in his mouth and made himself think about something else. He studied the table, bleached almost white by many scrubbings with lye water—he wondered if that was part of Rose Barker's job. Finding her in a place like this had surprised and disturbed him. With the money that he had sent her over the past ten years she could have bought the place.

A young boy with the heady aroma of a stable hand about him entered the dining room and looked at Tragg.

"You must be the one," he said, eying Tragg's clothing with amusement. "The sheriff says fetch you. He wants to talk to you."

All eyes turned toward Tragg. They hadn't trusted him in the first place, anybody wearin' such a rig. Now they were sure there was something wrong with him. Tragg sat back for a moment, trying to think what the sheriff might want to see him about. Nothing occurred to him, and he rejected the impulse to discuss it with the stableboy. "All right," he said, pushing his plate back willingly.

Apparently Jessie Ross had been listening at the door. She met Tragg when he came out and asked, "What's the sheriff want?"

Tragg gave her a bleak look and walked on. But Jessie was not an easy woman to ignore. She fell in beside him. "You goin' to ask him about that old Mex?"

"No."

"Then I'll just go along with you and we'll both talk to him." She didn't look at Callahan who was lounging on a fire barrel on the other side of the street, but she knew that he was watching her. "Tragg," she said quietly, "I think there's goin' to be trouble."

"What kind of trouble?"

". . . I ain't sure. A rider fogged into town while you was talkin' to the boardin' house cook. There was some palaver over at the hotel where the sheriff is. Then the sheriff sent that boy to fetch you . . ." She shrugged. "It all seems pretty queer." When Tragg made no reply, she said, "I *knew* there was a reason for you takin' a bounty. It was to give it to that woman, wasn't it?"

Tragg shot her a poisonous look which she chose to

ignore. "So that was Rose Barker," she went on dreamily, as if she were thinking out loud to herself. "What was it, Tragg? Before he died, did Jody Barker make you promise to look after her?"

Tragg's face was stiff with anger. "Well," she went on, "I told you before that you're not the only one that might have a reason for takin' a bounty. Would you believe it if I told you that Coly *wanted* me to do just what I'm doin'?"

Tragg stared at her. "He wanted you to turn him in, knowin' he'd be charged with murder?"

"Coly's got a bullet in his lungs. He's good as dead, anyway."

Curiously, Tragg found himself believing her. A man who had nothing to lose could afford to be generous. If Jody Barker could do it, so could Coly Brown.

Sheriff Max Ellender was feverish, ill tempered, and in pain, but he ignored his own misery for a moment when Tragg entered the room. "How'd you make out with Rose Barker?"

"Is that the reason you sent for me?" Tragg said stiffly.

"No. Just thought I'd ask." Ellender laughed dryly. "Hates your guts, don't she?"

"I killed her husband."

The sheriff gestured wearily, waving the notion away. "Doin' your duty. Jody Barker was a killer. Had to be stopped." He lay for a moment, his eyes closed. "Tragg, I need your help."

Tragg was instantly wary. "What kind of help?"

"Recollect the sodbuster that killed the cowhand and the driver?"

"We don't know that he killed them."

Ellender snorted. "Don't be a fool. He killed the cow-hand and the driver, and now he's killed a cowman." He opened his eyes and gazed at Tragg. "Omar Jessup. Not very important when you stack him up against some of the big cowmen up in the Panhandle, but important enough down here. Especially to the hands that worked for him. You understand what I'm gettin' at?"

"I don't see what it has to do with me."

"I need a deputy. My own deputy's out there on the prairie, God knows where." He saw Tragg's jaw come up at a stubborn angle. "Before you start tellin' me my business, just listen to me a minute. The sodbuster's in bad trouble. Right now half of Jessup's hands are trackin' him down, and the other half is lookin' for a tree tall enough to hang him on." He glared for a moment, and the room hummed with silence. "I don't care about the sodbuster," he said harshly. "I understand what happened to him and why he killed Jessup, but I don't give a damn. What I'm interested in is a bunch of good cowhands that have got it in their heads to lynch him. I've never had a lynchin' in this county. After all this time, I don't aim to let the habit get started."

"I know how you feel," Tragg told him, "but there's nothin' I can do."

Ellender regarded him with distaste. "That's where you're wrong. You can pin on a deputy's badge and ride out to the Jessup place and put a stop to this business before it's too late."

"How do you know it's not already too late?"

"I don't. But one of the Jessup hands just rode in to tell

me about Omar. The sodbuster was still loose when he left the outfit."

Tragg shook his head. "This ain't my county. How could I be a deputy?"

"If you take the badge from me, that's enough. There's damn few men in this county," he added coldly, "that'll give you any trouble on that score."

It was easy to believe him. Sick or well, Max Ellender was not a man who would often have his word or intentions questioned. But Tragg shook his head a second time. "It's out of the question."

"Why? After ten years of wearin' tasseled huntin' shirts, have you lost your nerve?"

Anger appeared in two flaming spots on Tragg's cheeks. The two men glared at each other with dislike but not with distrust. After a long silence, Tragg asked, "What reason did Morrasey have for killin' the cowman?"

Ellender lay back on his damp pillow, knowing that he was going to get his way. "The sodbuster—Morrasey— struck north a few weeks ago to look for work. Left his woman on the place. Well . . ." He gestured limply. "I guess you know what it's like for a woman, by herself, on a quarter section of rocks and clay. No water. Damn little grub. Nobody to talk to . . ."

"What happened?" Tragg pressed.

The sheriff spread his hands. "One day she just went off and laid down and died. It's not the first time it's happened."

"Where does the cowman Jessup come into it?"

"Jessup . . ." Ellender seemed to sigh without actually doing so. "Jessup was a cowman. Tough, but fair with his own men. When it came to sodbusters it was a different story. At the beginning, Morrasey had a creek-bottom place, but Omar and his boys run him off. Morrasey had to move up to higher ground—he never had no chance of growin' crops in ground like that. Well, when the sodbuster got home and found out his woman was dead—it was easy enough, I guess, to lay the blame at Jessup's feet."

"Did anybody actually *see* Morrasey kill Jessup?"

The sheriff shook his head. "That's one reason the lynchin' has to be stopped. Oh, he killed him, all right. There's no question about that. But it might not be easy to prove in court—especially if there was a sodbuster on the jury. Anyhow, we've got a circuit judge hereabouts that's hell on lynchin'." He closed his eyes again, making a great effort to gather his thoughts. "Tragg, these cowhands are friends of mine. Pretty soon, if they're not stopped, they're goin' to be killers. Then, as soon as my leg mends, I'll have to go after them and haul them in and see them hung. I don't want that."

Threats alone would not have changed Tragg's mind, they would only have hardened his original stand. But this frank appeal to help the sheriff do his job was another matter. Tragg felt his resistance crumbling. "If I *did* go out and find Morrasey and bring him back here, what would happen to him?"

"I don't know." The sheriff didn't look at Tragg. He didn't even open his eyes. "Maybe nothin'."

Tragg didn't believe it for an instant. He surprised himself more than the sheriff when he said, "If you want to swear me in, I'll see what I can do."

For a moment Ellender said nothing. Then he nodded

toward the oak dresser and sighed. "It won't be an easy job. Bring me that tablet and pencil and I'll try to show you how the different spreads are laid out in this county." Tragg handed him the tablet of ruled paper and a lead pencil. The sheriff sketched the major landmarks, the streams and ridges, and great expanses of flat prairie. He marked an X in the lower left-hand corner of the paper. "Here is the Jessup headquarters. There's permanent line camps over here and over here. There's other outfits down south on the Colorado, but I'm hopin' you won't have to deal with them. Morrasey's place, best I can recollect, is somewheres around here." He made another X west of Jessup's headquarters. "I can furnish you with a horse and rifle, but I can't send anybody with you. Everybody in the county's either a cowman or sodbuster. Or a storekeeper that don't give a damn." Suddenly his eyes were clear and sharp. "Like I say, findin' Morrasey and haulin' him in won't be easy. You figger you can do it?"

"I don't know. It's been almost ten years."

"Well . . ." The sheriff allowed himself a small, humorless smile. "It's like ridin' horseback, they say. If you was ever any good at it, you don't forget."

Jessie Ross was waiting in front of the hotel when Tragg came out. "What did the sheriff want?"

Tragg made an impatient sound and started to shove past her. But the young woman was not to be shaken off so easily. "Was it about Morrasey? The sodbuster that killed the cowman?"

Tragg stopped in his tracks. "How'd you know about that?"

"Everybody in town knows. There's a cowhand over at the saloon tellin' everybody that'll listen."

Tragg groaned involuntarily. Jessie Ross, a young woman who liked to stick to business, asked, "Did you talk to the sheriff about the bounty?"

"No." Tragg started toward the livery barn with Jessie still at his side.

"Why didn't you?" she demanded indignantly.

"It's none of my business."

"Goin' out to hunt for that crazy sodbuster's none of your business, either, and you'll likely get yourself shot in the bargain. But you're doin' it."

Tragg walked faster, hoping to pull away. But Jessie grabbed his arm and hung on. "I guess I can talk to the sheriff myself. Most likely he'll want part of the bounty money—but it might be worth it, if he can keep Callahan away from me."

"The sheriff's in no shape to help anybody, or he wouldn't have made me a deputy."

"Well," she accused him, "I sure can't depend on *you* to help me."

Tragg looked at her, and some of his distaste must have shown in his expression, for her face flushed unexpectedly as she released his arm. "Funny," she said in a small voice, genuinely hurt, "I thought you'd understand how it was with me and Coly. You of all people. I mean, there was a time when you wasn't too good to take a bounty."

"That was different."

". . . Was it?" Uncowed, still as proud as a young Comanche, she wheeled and marched away.

Tragg sighed. He hadn't meant to hurt her. That,

according to some of his old friends, was Tragg's trouble. He never meant to hurt anyone. A man like that never should have been a lawman, they said. And maybe they were right.

But here he was starting it all over again. For reasons which were not even his own.

CHAPTER SEVEN

MORRASEY wandered numbly along the dry wash, dragging the polished stock of Jessup's saddle rifle in the dirt. He had been walking most of the day—walking, running, hiding. His tongue was thick from thirst, his throat gritty. At last he left the dry gully and came to one of Jessup's earth cattle tanks. He fell face down in the red mud and gulped the green-scummed water.

He lay for a while beside that stagnant pond, listening to the soft rush of wind through the brown grass. "Cow country," he thought bleakly. Farmers killed their mules and broke their plows just trying to turn the sod. A brief rage seized him. It was unfair! Even the land itself fought on the side of the cowmen!

I never should of come here, he thought. I never should of brought Delly away from her people.

But he shoved these thoughts to the back of his mind, and he slammed the door on them and locked it. He had been trying to make a better life for Delly. That was why he had left Kansas. A dry and bitter land he had left. But in Kansas, at least, the cowmen hadn't fenced off the water. A farmer, with hard work and a little luck, could make a living. And he could have made a living here, too, except for cowmen like Omar Jessup.

With grim pleasure Morrasey let his thoughts dwell on Jessup. But even that pleasure soon went sour. As they always did, his thoughts returned to Delly, and to that mound of raw clay.

He lay there for a long while in the gummy mud. Two of Jessup's riders, quartering toward Dead Man's Creek, passed less than a hundred yards away. Morrasey crawled to the rim of the dirt tank and watched them over the barrel of the saddle gun. I'd kill the both of them. If they'd just come closer.

But Morrasey knew that he was not a "gunman." Up to now his killing had been mostly luck. So the two cowhands rode on, unaware that death had reached out to take them, and then had shrugged and passed them by. There was a time when Morrasey had been able to shoot rabbits and squirrels with a rifle. But shooting men was different. Rabbits and squirrels ran for their holes when your bullet missed them. Men were apt to shoot back.

He realized that one of Jessup's hands had probably found the dead cowman by this time; more than likely someone had gone to Bosen's Grove to inform the sheriff. It was even possible that the bodies of the stage driver and the young cowhand had been discovered. Most likely the sheriff already had a posse looking for him.

Morrasey felt the sweat forming on his forehead. He looked at his hands and they were trembling. He could almost feel the rough touch of hemp on his throat. They would call it murder. Nobody in cow country ever listened to a sodbuster. They would call it murder and string him up to the nearest tree. If they caught him.

If they caught him.

He lurched to his feet, clawed his way out of the tank, and began to run.

It seemed to Morrasey that he had been running for days. He lay on his back in a stand of weeds and stared up at the blinding sun. How far he had come or in what direction he had no idea. He only knew that he could go no longer. His legs would no longer support him. His lungs were on fire.

He turned his head and closed his eyes to shut out the sun. The next thing he knew it was night. He was cold and stiff and damp with dew. He got up and walked some more, dragging the rifle. He thought about the posse that was probably looking for him, and about Jessup's hands, and what they would do to him if they caught him.

And even as he thought about these things a crushing indifference bore down on him. It was as if his store of panic had been exhausted. Not even the prospect of hanging had the power to frighten him. "I'm good as dead," he thought aloud. "I know it."

His head was clear. He was even able to see a kind of grim humor in his predicament. He considered it as a kind of enormous joke on the Creator—for he had never really been alive. Save for that brief time in Kansas, before he had made his fatal decision to bring Delly to Texas.

He walked all that morning, making vaguely for the old military road to Fort Belknap. The road was used mostly by freighters now, and sometimes peddlers and tinkers who traveled the huge circuit of ranch headquarters. Once again Morrasey was acutely aware of the money belt around his middle. If he could reach the road there was a chance that he could bribe someone to take him out of the county and maybe even sell him a saddle horse. For a man with money there was always hope.

Owen Tragg, consulting Sheriff Ellender's map of the county, reached the Jessup headquarters around mid-morning. An old wrangler hobbled out of a feed shed and stared at him in sour belief. He glanced at the badge on Tragg's tasseled hunting shirt.

"Where's the sheriff? The boys figgered to have him here for the hangin', soon's they catch that murderin' sod-buster."

Tragg explained about Ellender's broken leg. "Where is everybody?"

"Over west somewheres, waitin' for the dogs." Tragg's clothing fascinated him. He shook his head in disapproval. "Where the hell'd you ever find a rig like that, anyhow?"

Tragg grinned faintly. The question had been put to him many times but he had never been able to think of a suit-able answer. "What's this about dogs?"

"Jed Purdy's wolfhounds. How come Ellender didn't deputize one of the boys in town? What we want out here's a lawman, not a medicine-show doctor."

Tragg's smile was like a razor scratch across his face. "Much oblige for the information." He reined to the west and rode away from the wrangler's sneering shrug.

He could hear the dogs for several minutes before he actually saw them. Then, on topping a rise, he could see the cowhands gathered around a stone outcrop. One of the hands was holding four spotted wolfhounds on leashes, and the dogs were jumping and barking and snapping at each other in excitement.

Four of the cowhands were hunkered down against the outcrop, smoking. The fifth hand was trying without success to silence the dogs. A sixth man was riding toward the group from the south. Still a good distance away, the horsebacker waved something over his head. The man with the dogs turned and nodded to his friends.

All hands got to their feet when they saw Tragg. They stared at him, looked at one another, then stared again. In their expressions was the same sneering derision that Tragg had already encountered with the wrangler. They watched him in frank disbelief, but their immediate mission was too sober a matter to allow for outright laughter.

"What the hell?" one of the hands said in unfocused anger.

"Ain't that a badge I see amongst all the tassels and doodads?"

Even the dogs quieted their yelping and snapping long enough to cast curious looks at the stranger. "Well now," one of the hands said sourly as Tragg rode into hearing range, "what do you boys guess we got here?"

The five faces were hostile and humorless as Tragg reined his borrowed animal to a halt. Tragg sighed to himself but spoke quietly. "The name's Tragg. Sheriff Ellender's back in town with a busted leg. It was his notion to give me this badge. It's my job now to help you look for the man that killed your boss."

"Ellender must of busted his head along with his leg," one of the hands said flatly.

There were a few fleeting, halfhearted grins. Then another hand, who spoke with a ring of authority, stepped forward. "We don't need any help findin' Morrasey. The dogs'll do that for us." He nodded toward the approaching rider. "There comes Red from Morrasey's shack with a piece of the sodbuster's duds. Let the hounds know just who it is they're after."

Tragg nodded blandly. "That's fine. I'll just ride along and take Morrasey back to town when you locate him."

They looked at him with slitted eyes. "Take him back to town," one of the hands echoed dryly. Someone snickered.

"Takin' him to town ain't quite what we had in mind," the leader said contemptuously. "You ride back to Bosen's Grove, Tragg, and tell Ellender we'll take care of things ourselves. We don't need any fancy-rigged dude to help us."

Tragg could feel the heat of anger creeping into his face, but he remained silent until he was sure that he could speak calmly. "If you string Morrasey up, the sheriff will have you tried for murder. He wanted me to tell you that."

The leader smiled coldly. "Let him. There ain't a cowman in the county that wouldn't let us go."

"What about squatters?"

"Sodbusters don't serve on juries."

"This time," Tragg said evenly, "they might. If you make Ellender sore enough."

Obviously this possibility had never crossed the leader's mind.

"Mister," he said after a thoughtful silence, "I don't know who you are, or why Max Ellender gave you that badge to wear along with all your other bangles, but this is one job we aim to see to ourselves. You can go back to town and tell Ellender."

After ten years of talking nonsense from a lecture platform, Tragg had almost forgotten how hardheaded people could be when you tried to talk sense to them. He crossed his hands on the saddle horn and studied the faces one by one. "Revenge is a satisfyin' thing sometimes—but is it worth hangin' for? Are you men ready for that?"

The cowhand known as Red rode up to the grim-faced gathering. He stared at Tragg for several seconds, then asked, "Who're you?"

Patiently, Tragg explained who he was and how he came to be acting as Sheriff Ellender's deputy. "Are you the boss here?" he asked the self-appointed leader.

"Foreman. Used to be, when Omar Jessup was alive."

"You'd better talk some sense to these men. The sheriff won't stand for lynchin'."

"If the sheriff's got a busted leg, he'll have a hard time stoppin' us."

"He put that job up to me."

The foreman smiled faintly. Like the others, he found Tragg's rig amusing, but the smile faded when he came to the gray coolness of the deputy's eyes. "You're not fool enough to try to stop us, are you?"

". . . I might be."

The cowman looked at him and seemed to sigh. Suddenly Red kneed his animal against Tragg's leg. The dogs, sensing the excitement, again started jumping and barking. All the hands had caught the foreman's signal. All of them came at Tragg at the same time. Somebody grabbed his reins. Someone else had grabbed his off leg and was hauling him down from the saddle. Even as he kicked and thrashed about, Tragg had to admire their efficiency.

Tragg made his first serious mistake when he grabbed for his saddle rifle. One of the men smashed his hand with a gun barrel. He fell out of the saddle and landed heavily on his shoulder. "See if he's got a pistol amongst all that buckskin fringe," the foreman was saying quietly.

Tragg made his second serious mistake; he tried to drag his revolver out of his holster. "Watch him, Bob!" Red said sharply.

"I see him," Bob said coolly.

At that moment a sharp-toed boot kicked the .45 out of Tragg's hand. Then his head seemed to explode as the cowhand called Red loomed over him and slashed with his own heavy revolver.

The foreman said calmly, "That's enough." But Tragg had already sunk beneath the waves of darkness by that time.

Brian Callahan had taken up a position next to a fire barrel, in front of Bosen's Grove's only general store. He had a good view of the hotel's front door and the outside stairway. He had been watching the building with unblinking interest ever since Jessie Ross had entered it a few minutes before. Everybody in Bosen's Grove, including Callahan, knew that the sheriff was laid up in the hotel with a broken leg, and Callahan guessed rightly that the Ross woman was now getting the necessary details on how to collect the bounty money on Coly Brown.

All this suited Callahan perfectly. It meant that half the bounty would soon be his. Maybe all of it. Depending on how frightened Jessie was of Coly's pals. Callahan smiled to himself, lit a stubby cigar, and made himself comfortable. The stage fare from Dodge City to Bosen's Grove had cleaned out his meager bank roll, but he was now satisfied that the gamble would be won.

Jessie Ross came out of the hotel, and Callahan was instantly alert. He crossed the street and headed her off as she made for the boardinghouse. "Everything all set with the sheriff? He don't figger to cut hisself in on that scalp money, does he?"

She raked him with an icy gaze. Callahan laughed. "You don't really need any help from that sheriff. The reward's no business of his."

"It's his county."

"Sure," Callahan said grinning, "but I been nosin' around down at the wagon yard. Old Valona's headquarters ain't but a day's ride from here. We could rent a rig and drive over there and collect the bounty, just the two of us. Wouldn't anybody else know."

It was Jessie's turn to smile. She could see herself coming back from Valona's place with Callahan, with ten thousand dollars between them. She'd wind up along the road as coyote bait, and Callahan would take the first stage to Dodge with the full bounty in his pocket. This was why she wanted to make it all as legal as possible.

Callahan was watching her, still smiling. "Well? Is the sheriff goin' to haul the old Mex into Bosen's Grove where you can talk to him?"

Jessie set her jaw stubbornly and walked on. Suddenly Callahan spat out his cigar. He grabbed her arm in a viselike grip and snarled under his breath. "Listen to me! All I have to do is open my mouth and the whole yarn'll get back to Coly and his pals. Where do you think you'd be then?"

Jessie felt her arm going numb. But Callahan, unlike some of the men who rode with Coly Brown, had not had Kiowa instruction in the art of torture. A mere arm twisting was a light caress compared with what she could expect from them.

"What," Callahan demanded, "went on in that hotel between you and the sheriff? Is he bringin' the old Mex or ain't he?"

"Let go my arm!" There were tears in her eyes that she couldn't blink away.

Callahan eased his grip. "How long's it goin' to be before you get the money?"

She hesitated. Callahan's grip tightened. "I don't know! The sheriff said he'd get word to the old man. The rest would be up to me."

"What does that mean?"

"I tell the old man where to find Coly. When he's sure I told him the truth, he'll give me the money."

Callahan scowled. "A thing like that could take a month or longer."

"Not the way the sheriff tells it. The old man's got connections in Kansas. All he has to do is get to a telegraph and tell them."

Callahan's grin widened. "Then Valona's friends find Coly and kill him, and that's the end of it? You get the money?"

She looked down at the ground. "I guess."

He let her arm go and rubbed his hands together, like a man who has just done a good day's work. "The whole thing oughtn't take more'n a week or so. Then we'll split the bounty, you go your way and I'll go mine."

Two or three curious citizens of Bosen's Grove had come out on the sidewalk to watch the bizarre little scene in front of the hotel. Callahan said quietly, "Don't get it in your head that you can slip away from me. Is that plain?"

She nodded.

Callahan tipped his hat politely to Jessie Ross, smiled widely at the townsmen, then sauntered back to the other side of the street.

It was several minutes later that Callahan approached the boardinghouse where Jessie Ross had taken a room. A small, prune of a woman met him on the front porch. "Supper," she told him snappishly, "won't be on the table till five o'clock."

Callahan smiled pleasantly. "What I'm lookin' for is a room."

She was instantly suspicious. Men usually stayed at the wagon yard, except for a few drummers and Sheriff Ellender who put up at the hotel. The boardinghouse was usually thought of as a refuge for lone women who had got themselves stranded, for one reason or another, in Bosen's Grove. "Have you tried the wagon yard?"

Callahan spread his hands in a gesture of helplessness. "Camp shacks all filled. I was with the stage that broke down on the road."

She nodded grudgingly. "All right. There's a sleepin' porch out back. The cook'll show you. No licker and no smokin'. Half a dollar a night."

Callahan bowed and smiled. He picked up his grip and entered the big dining room. Swirling heat mingled with the smell of cooking. The place seemed deserted. He walked through to the kitchen and called, "Anybody here?"

An iron pot simmered on the stove. Fresh bread had recently been taken from the oven and laid out on the cook table to cool. Callahan called again, and again received no response. He had started back to the dining room when he became aware of the watchful eyes.

She was sitting hunched over on the rickety stairway that led to the boardinghouse's three main rent rooms. She must have been there all along, listening as Callahan talked to the old woman, watching as he entered the house and walked back to the kitchen. She must have heard him calling. Callahan looked at her for a moment, scowling. "You the cook here?"

She didn't move or make a sound, but she looked at him so intently that Callahan's skin began to crawl. At first glance she seemed a classic model of a High Plains woman—dry, colorless, the juice of life long since worked out of her. Her age might have been anything between twenty and forty—a very old twenty or a sun-cured forty. Lank strands of lifeless hair stuck to her moist forehead. Her face was lined and rough enough to strike matches on. Only those washed-out eyes were thoroughly alive.

Callahan shrugged off a certain uneasiness and said, "The old woman said you'd show me to the sleepin' porch. But I guess I can find it myself."

She asked surprisingly, "You know who I am?"

". . . No, ma'am. Unless you're the cook, like the old woman said."

"Rose Barker," she said tonelessly. "The name mean anything to you?"

110

Callahan stared at her thoughtfully. "There used to be a Jody Barker. He had a woman, so I've heard."

"I was Jody's woman." She watched him like a circling hawk watching a field mouse. Suddenly she got to her feet and descended the stairs. "I'll show you the sleepin' porch."

He followed her through the kitchen to a screened-in porch built to the back of the house. Its only furniture was an iron cot with a grass mattress, and a corner washstand. It suited Callahan fine; at least it would be cooler than an ordinary room. He set his grip on the floor and mopped his forehead. When he turned, Rose Barker was still standing in the doorway, watching him.

"What is it?" he asked in irritation. "We never met anywhere before now, have we?"

"No." She shook her head. "But there used to be some men . . . They'd come around sometimes to talk to Jody, and I'd see them. You remind me of them."

"What men? Who were they?"

"I don't know their names."

"What kind of men were they?"

"They were killers."

A ringing silence rose up between them as they stared at one another. Loco, Callahan thought to himself. Just another squatter woman that lost her man in a hostile country and went a little out of her head. He managed an uneasy laugh. "Sorry, ma'am, you must have me mixed up with somebody else. I'm just a plain man. Sure never set myself up as a gunsharp or anything like that."

"Maybe." But she didn't sound as if she believed it. "You remind me of them, though. And they were killers."

Without as much as a nod, she turned and walked away.

Callahan sat heavily on the bunk. "Loco," he said aloud, as if he were hoping to convince himself of that fact. In defiance of the old woman's ban against smoking, he drew a cigar from his shirt pocket and lit it.

He soon decided that he didn't care so much for this sleeping porch after all. It was too open. He was too vulnerable here. If it hadn't been for the necessity of keeping an eye on Jessie Ross he would have moved somewhere else.

He decided that for the moment he could watch the boardinghouse from the saloon across the street. As he tramped back through the steaming kitchen, Rose Barker turned from the stove and looked at him.

"Hot," Callahan said, with an attempt at good humor.

She said nothing, except with her eyes. Callahan tramped on out of the house, relieved to breathe the free air of the street again.

At five o'clock sharp the ancient little proprietress of the boardinghouse banged an iron triangle at the corner of the front porch. Immediately the storekeepers began locking their doors. The citizenry of Bosen's Grove drifted into the street and straggled in ones and twos toward the town's only self-confessed eating house. A few of the hardier ones, and the poorer ones, stayed back and ate their own cooking, or took whatever was available in the saloons. But most of the town headed for the boardinghouse, Callahan with them.

Callahan lounged on the front porch with several others, waiting for the second table. Jessie Ross, being the only woman guest, was taking her supper in her room, but Callahan wasn't aware of this. When she did not appear with the first group of diners, and still did not make an appearance with the second table, he began to worry. What if she had given him the slip in spite of his watchfulness? What if she had managed to meet with old Valona or one of his men and make her own bargain?

It didn't seem likely. Still, he became restless, and when she did not appear with the stragglers who made up the third and final table of the day, he started for the kitchen, in search of the old woman who owned the place. He found Rose Barker.

She had been watching him again, this time from the kitchen doorway. "I was lookin' for Miss Ross," he said impatiently.

She looked at him blankly.

"One of the passengers in the coach that broke down," Callahan went on. "When she didn't come down to supper, I began to wonder."

A flicker of understanding showed in those faded eyes. "Took her supper upstairs," she said. "Women boarders do that sometimes."

Callahan was relieved. He even managed a small smile. Rose Barker said quietly, "How much does it cost to kill a man?"

Callahan froze. The quiet conversational way she had put the question made his scalp prickle. He looked at her sharply to make sure that she was serious—and he knew instantly that there was no doubt on that score. Callahan found that his mouth was uncomfortably dry. "What kind of a question is that?" he demanded.

But the ring of indignation was flat. Rose Barker smiled. "There's a man I want killed. I want to know how much you'll charge."

"Look!" Callahan hissed angrily. "I don't know what you're up to and I don't know who you think I am, but I ain't goin' to . . ."

The protest ended abruptly in midsentence. Rose Barker had quietly reached into the deep pocket of her apron and drew out a roll of greenbacks. "I ain't askin' you to do it for nothin'," she said in a tone of utmost reasonableness. "I've got the money to pay you; just tell me how much."

Callahan stared hungrily at the money.

Rose Barker dropped the roll back in her apron pocket. "I'll talk to you later, when I've finished the supper dishes." Callahan blinked and shook himself, like a man coming out of a deep sleep. Then, in a quiet and thoughtful tone, he said, "It must be that fancy marshal, Tragg. He's the one that killed Jody Barker, they say." He looked at her closely. "Is it Tragg you want killed?"

She smiled, but Callahan was quick to note that the expression never reached her eyes. "We'll talk later. When I've finished in the kitchen."

"Where?"

"Out of doors somewheres. People're nosy, and those walls're thin."

"All right. Around the back of the house. I'll be waitin'." Callahan returned to the sleeping porch. "I'll be damned," he said quietly, wonderingly, to himself. "I'll *just* be damned." For a long while he sat on the cot smoking a cigar, listening to the whirring June flies in the bushes. Callahan had turned his hand to many things in his lifetime, but he had never taken up the trade of an assassin. Not that he had anything against it, particularly. No one had ever made him an offer before.

He had no intention of forgetting about Jessie Ross, just because this second opportunity had come along, but he could see no reason why he couldn't dispose of Tragg and still be on hand when Jessie collected the bounty for betraying Coly Brown. "Women," he thought with a wry, humorless grin.

He returned to the saloon across the street and killed time until night had settled like a silent blanket over Bosen's Grove. The street was almost deserted. Callahan took his bottle of St. Louis beer out to the plank sidewalk in front of the saloon and sniffed the thin, dust-spiced air of the High Plains. Yes sir, he thought with heavy satisfaction, the Callahan luck was sure enough beginning to change.

Down the street, in the direction of the wagon yard, an oblong of yellow light glowed hotly in the night. That would be the Spartan room of Sheriff Max Ellender, where that lawman was no doubt tossing fitfully and wondering if his special deputy was doing the job he had been sent to do, or if the time would soon come when the sheriff would be faced with the grim task of hanging his friends for the murder of a squatter.

In her small room over the boardinghouse kitchen, Jessie Ross gazed at the night and dreamed bleakly of days that might have been, if times had been different, or if she and Coly Brown had been different kinds of people.

In the sweltering kitchen of the boardinghouse, Rose

Barker finished washing and drying the supper dishes. This was the time that she had waited ten years for, and she tasted it and savored it as if it were heady wine.

And out on the prairie, to the west of Bosen's Grove, Owen Tragg knelt beside a trickle of gyp water and gingerly sponged the matting of dried blood from the side of his head.

Somewhere to the south, Frank Morrasey paused beside the same sluggish stream to get his breath, and that was when he first heard the excited baying of Jed Purdy's prized wolfhounds.

Callahan recrossed the street and picked his way toward the dark bulk of a lilac bush where Rose Barker was waiting. The boardinghouse reared like a sheer dark cliff behind them, with a single lamp burning dimly in one of the upstairs rooms. Rose Barker turned toward Callahan. "Well?"

Callahan went straight to the point. "Who do you want killed and how much can you afford to pay?"

"Owen Tragg," she said without hesitation. "I'll pay you . . . two hundred dollars."

Callahan chuckled quietly. "Gettin' on close to bedtime," he said dryly. He touched his hatbrim in a burlesque of gentility. "Good night, ma'am."

"What's the matter?" she asked in alarm.

"Two hundred dollars is what's the matter," he told her coldly. "The widow of Jody Barker ought to know better than that."

"How much then?"

". . . Two thousand."

She sucked her breath in sharply. "You're out of your head! Where would I get so much money?"

"That's what I've been wonderin' ever since you showed me the greenbacks."

"There wasn't nothin' like two thousand dollars there."

"Maybe . . . but it was enough to make me wonder." Suddenly he grinned. "Tragg," he said, thinking out loud. "It's just the kind of stunt he'd pull, I bet. He's been sendin' you money all along, hasn't he, since the time he killed Jody?"

Her voice turned razor sharp. "Money can't bring Jody back."

He was on solid ground, now that he knew just what kind of woman he was dealing with. He could even appreciate the irony of using Tragg's own money to pay for his assassination. "I got to hand it to you, ma'am," he said pleasantly, "you know how to hate. But it's still goin' to cost two thousand dollars."

She turned away and he could not see her face, but he could hear her heavy breathing. "Five hundred."

Callahan grinned. "Let's be reasonable, ma'am. The commonest kind of association gunslingers get that much for shootin' down sodbusters. Tragg ain't no sodbuster, he's a deputy marshal. That makes a difference."

"Tragg ain't been a marshal for ten years."

Callahan shrugged. "You know what I mean."

". . . A thousand dollars. It's all I've got in the world."

"Fifteen hundred," Callahan said comfortably. "Think about it for a minute. You've been ten years wantin' Tragg dead, and this is the first time he's even come close enough to look at. How many more chances do you think you'll get if you miss this one?"

She turned on him in cold anger, but after a moment she dropped her chin in reluctant agreement. "All right. You'll get it when the job is done."

"Half now," Callahan corrected, "the rest when Tragg is dead."

"Five hundred now," she said icily. "The rest when I see Tragg laid out."

Callahan sighed in resignation. "You drive a hard bargain, ma'am."

"It is a bargain, then?"

Callahan considered. "It's a bargain. But there's one thing I want to be sure about. How much do you remember about your time with Jody Barker?"

"I remember every minute of it."

"Then you'll remember Jody's pals. The 'killers' that you mentioned when we talked earlier today. You'll remember they wasn't the kind of men to take the short end of a bargain like this one."

She regarded him coldly. "Are you threatenin' to kill me if I don't pay you everything we've settled on?"

"Yes, ma'am. That's just what I'm doin'."

She surprised him by smiling. A smile as cold as a crack on a frozen pond, but still a smile. "That sounds fair enough. When . . . will it be?"

"Now seems like good a time as any. The sheriff down with a busted leg, and Tragg puttin' his nose in things that ain't any of his business."

She dropped the tight, thick roll of bills in his hand. "That seals the bargain."

"Five hundred dollars?"

"Count it if you want to," she said.

But Callahan stuffed the money in his pocket. "I'll count it later." The bargain was sealed. The job of killing Owen Tragg was his.

They talked on for a few more minutes, suspicious and reluctant partners that they now were, each afraid that the other would somehow worm out of his end of the agreement. "I'll let you know when it's done," he said at last.

"I'll know when I see Tragg laid out for buryin'."

With that, Rose Barker wheeled and walked into the night. Callahan remained a while longer, absently lighting a cigar. He smiled to himself. All in all, his trip from Dodge was proving to be a profitable one indeed.

But if he could have seen the rigid figure in the dark window that overlooked his sleeping porch, his smile might not have been so complacent.

As the sun came up the next morning Sheriff Max Ellender slept feverishly in his sweltering room at the hotel. Rose Barker was putting pans of biscuits into the oven in preparation for the first table at breakfast, as she had done almost every morning for the past ten years.

In her room on the second floor of the boardinghouse, Jessie Ross was wide awake and nervously pacing the floor, silently struggling with a matter of conscience.

Brian Callahan stood on the front porch of the boardinghouse enjoying his first cigar of the day. The strange scene with Rose Barker was unreal in his mind, but there was nothing unreal about the roll of greenbacks that he had carefully packed away in his grip.

When he finished his cigar he walked to the livery barn where the hostler was cleaning stalls. "What have you got in the way of rent animals?"

The hostler indicated the corral where a gray, two roans, and a black nuzzled their morning feed. The two roans were big gutted and spindle legged. Grays were not to be trusted. Callahan indicated that he would take the black. He went back to the barn and paid for two days and, being a stranger in town, left a deposit.

As he conducted this common bit of business Callahan began to get the uncomfortable feeling that he was being watched. As he was settling his rent rig on the black, he wheeled suddenly toward the street.

Jessie Ross was watching him from in front of a harness shop. She had left the boardinghouse and, even before the storekeepers had opened for business, had followed him the length of the town's single street. And there she stood, like a blanket Indian, expressionless, watching his every move.

Callahan found the experience strangely disturbing. For days now he had been following her, dogging her foot-steps, hardly letting her out of his sight. Now, for some reason, the situation had reversed itself. She was following and watching *him*.

Scowling, he led the black toward the nearby harness shop. "What're you lookin' at? What do you want?"

She studied him thoughtfully. "I had my window up last night. I heard you and Jody Barker's widow talkin'."

Callahan flushed with irritation, but it was no more than that. After all, they had much in common, he and Jessie Ross. "All right," he conceded, "you heard. Go back to the boardin'house and put it out of your mind."

"You're goin' to kill Tragg," she said. It was a quiet,

thoughtful statement, not a question.

"Go on back to the boardin'house," he said harshly.

"Why?" she asked. "Why do you have to kill Tragg?"

In the same harsh tone, he laughed. "For money, ma'am. Like everything else, for money."

"Ain't it enough that you'll get half the bounty when I kill Coly Brown?" She had never thought of it before as "killing" Coly, although that's what it would amount to.

"You never get enough money, ma'am," Callahan said with mock courtesy. "Now go on back to the boardin'-house." His tone was suddenly sharp. "And no tricks. I'll be back a long time before you get a chance to do any collectin'." She looked at him with disgust, but Callahan only smiled. "Don't you forget about them pals of Coly's and what they'll do to you if they find out you turned Coly in. You remember that and everything'll work out fine."

Jessie Ross was not likely to forget. All that night she had been remembering things, bits and pieces out of her life with Coly Brown. One incident in particular had stuck in her mind—it had started over a misunderstanding over a girl, or maybe it had been a poker game. Coly and his pals had bound the offending stranger hand and foot, and then they had made him a band of green rawhide for his head. That was all. They had ridden off and had never seen or heard of him again. Left him in the sun, with the shrinking rawhide band on his head. One of Coly's friends had figured it would take about four hours, maybe a little longer, for the band to shrink enough to pop the stranger's skull.

One day in the future there might be a rawhide band for her head. It was not likely that she would forget about that.

CHAPTER EIGHT

MORRASEY sat for some time listening to the distant baying of the hounds before he realized that they were after him. A lance of terror went through him. A good hound could track anything. A badger, a deer, a bear, a man. Unless the man was smarter than the hounds.

He began to run, but it soon became clear, even to a man in panic, that he could not outrun the dogs. He stopped and closed his eyes in furious concentration. Suddenly he began again to run, this time at a calculated gait, pacing himself, with a definite objective in mind. It would take more than a pack of dogs to track Frank Morrasey! he thought grimly. A lot more than that, boys!

He slanted to the east, jogging steadily now, not bothering to select a favorable terrain, not even bothering to look for animal tracks that might throw the dogs off momentarily. He jogged on in his sodbuster's ungainly lope which nevertheless devoured distance at a surprising rate.

He topped a rocky rise and pulled up for a moment, gazing bleakly at that patch of arid farmland that had once been his. That mound of red raw clay where Delly lay.

Despair and grief came down on him with the weight of an avalanche and threatened to crush him. But, in the end, hate was stronger. He shouldered aside the almost irresistible desire to drop there, as Delly had done, and give up. He made himself look away from that mound, and he loped doggedly on to the sod hut where all his hopes, and

Delly's, had died. Even before Delly herself had died.

But he didn't think about that now. He wouldn't let himself think about it. Grasping Jessup's rifle as if it were a club, he pounded on to the hut and fell into the doorway. There he remained for several minutes, getting his breath, staring at that sod house that he had hated so savagely, but nevertheless it had been the place where he and Delly had lived. And now it wrenched at his guts to think of leaving it.

He listened to the dogs as they veered far to the east on one of his old trails. They wouldn't stay on the old trail long. They'd find the latest one and, within a matter of minutes, the cowhands would be pounding at a full gallop toward the soddy.

In a sudden frenzy Morrasey fumbled among Delly's meager cooking supplies on a shelf over the stove. One of the small parcels he stuffed in his pocket. Then he breathed deeply three or four times. Again, with definite purpose, he began to run.

Along the sandy bottom of the dry wash behind the soddy he jogged with machine-like purpose. When the walls of that deep gully began to narrow steeply he stopped and opened the parcel that he had taken from the hut. With great care he dusted its contents along the bottom, laying a thin layer of reddish flakes over his tracks. When the parcel was empty he paused to study what he had done, and he was satisfied.

By the time the cowhands, led by the hounds, reached the sod hut, Morrasey was far to the south on another rocky slope. But he could hear the wild confusion of the dogs as they led the handler through the hut. After a time they picked up the latest scent, as Morrasey had known they would. He hunkered down in a stand of sunflower weeds, listening as the hounds bayed triumphantly, excitedly dragging their handler down the steep banks of the wash.

Just a little farther, Morrasey thought grimly. You pack of rich men's hounds that are so good at trackin' things. Just a little farther!

He smiled ever so faintly as the lead hound sniffed the dried chili flakes that Morrasey had left for him. The dog howled in pain and indignation, and the sound was followed almost immediately by all the hounds. That, he told himself with stolid satisfaction, took care of the dogs. The effect of powdered pepper in those sensitive nostrils would last for days, and in the meantime they would be worthless for tracking.

Morrasey did not try to convince himself that his troubles were over; he knew better than that. But at least he no longer had to worry about dogs.

In the distance Tragg had heard the dogs baying excitedly. Morrasey's done for, he thought bleakly. He listened for the spatter of rifle fire that inevitably followed the end of a hunt. This time it did not come. The hounds howled wildly for several minutes, then suddenly were quiet.

He didn't know what had happened, but the dogs had either lost the scent or had been taken away. Which could only mean they had captured Morrasey.

Tragg knelt beside the gyp-water stream and splashed more water on his wounded head. I'm not in any kind of shape to be a lawman, he told himself wearily. I'm too old, too soft. He doubted that even the greenest and youngest town marshal would have let himself be buffaloed by those cowhands.

He pushed himself to his feet, still listening for that last-minute flurry of rifle fire which did not come. Had the sod-buster escaped them after all? Had he somehow managed to throw the dogs off the trail?

Wincing, Tragg set his hat on his injured head and began plodding toward the south, in the direction that he had last heard the dogs. A fine lawman, he thought with bitter humor. No horse, no rifle. Only a single-action .45 that he had almost forgotten how to use.

That was when Tragg glimpsed Morrasey's gangling figure scrambling along the crest of a rise. It disappeared almost immediately on the other side.

Tragg knelt in some prairie weeds. Well, he thought, I'm still wearin' Ellender's badge. I guess that makes me a lawman . . . of sorts.

He studied the gentle slope, and the twisting green curve of Dead Man's Creek in the distance. The protective brush of that creek bottom was, no doubt, where Morrasey was headed. Crouching, Tragg began working his way toward the rise, hoping that Morrasey was much too occupied with the pursuing cowhands to notice what was happening behind him.

With the mincing, awkward gait of a horseman on foot, he made for the deceptively cool-looking creek bottom. He had come almost within revolver range of the heavy brush when that twangy, whiny voice that Tragg remembered so well, called, "Stop where you are, Tragg, or you're a dead man."

Tragg threw himself into a stand of mullein. "Listen to me, Morrasey. The sheriff at Bosen's Grove sent me to fetch you back for killin' Omar Jessup. He wants you alive, to stand trial."

"I bet!" Morrasey said with a high-pitched sneer.

"Alive, Morrasey. It's a better proposition than those cowhands will give you."

There was a moment of silence. Tragg went on with as much calm as he could muster. "I'm comin' on in, Morrasey. I can't stop you from usin' that rifle. But remember what I said about the cowhands."

He gave Morrasey a moment to consider the logic of his stand. Then he stood up in the green mullein, and rarely had he ever felt so naked. Holding his hand well away from his .45 he began walking.

"Morrasey?"

The sodbuster snarled, "Keep walkin'."

With a pounding head and an aching gut, Tragg walked the few remaining yards. It might have been the length of Texas, with some of Mexico thrown in, from the effort it took. He could not see the muzzle of the rifle, and the hatred in Morrasey's eyes. Morrasey stood up and motioned him to stop.

"This is your lucky day, Tragg!" he said in his snarling whine. "You don't know."

Tragg knew. His legs felt rubbery. His mouth was dry. Morrasey rammed the muzzle of the short-barreled rifle into Tragg's gut and took his .45. "Where's the cowhands with the dogs?"

". . . I don't know. I heard the dogs, then they stopped."

Surprisingly, Morrasey laughed. It was a sound that

made Tragg's skin itch. He motioned for the deputy to sit down. Then he bit off a small piece of twist tobacco and began to chew. "What you doin' here?" he asked at last.

As briefly as possible, Tragg explained about the sheriff's broken leg.

"You're a fool." Morrasey announced it as a simple fact.

"Look at the spot you're in," Tragg told him. "There's at least five cowhands lookin' for you right now. By sundown there'll be twenty more. Cowmen don't take kindly to havin' one of their own gunned down by a sodbuster."

Morrasey made his snarling sound. "Shut up! Let me think!"

"The two of us workin' together might just make it back to Bosen's Grove, before too many cowmen get in on the hunt."

"Shut up!" Morrasey snarled again. He squatted down on his heels, rocking moodily back and forth. "Where's your horse?" he asked after a time.

In an embarrassed tone Tragg confessed that he had lost his horse when the cowhands had buffaloed him.

Morrasey shot him a pitying look, as if to say, What can you expect? Anybody that would wear a rig like that! Then he went back to his moody chewing and rocking. "Well," he said, thinking out loud, "the dogs're done for. That'll slow the cowhands up a mite—trackin's slow business without dogs. But they might figger I headed for the creek. On account of the brush. Cowhands, from what I've seen of them, ain't right bright, but they might just figger that out." He spat a stream of tobacco juice in the weeds. "How," he asked—and there was a certain craftiness in his voice that immediately put Tragg on his guard, "do you aim to get us back to Bosen's Grove?"

Tragg held out his hand. "My gun first."

The sodbuster stopped his rocking and stared at him. Tragg went on calmly, "It's *you* the cowhands want to string up, not me. If you don't want my help . . ."

Morrasey's tone turned crafty again. "You might be right, at that. Bein' in jail ain't my notion of high livin', but I reckon it's better'n lookin' up a rope. You reckon," he asked blandly, "a sodbuster can get a fair trial in Bosen's Grove?"

". . . I don't know," Tragg answered frankly. "But I figger your chances are better there than here."

Morrasey's mouth twitched in a bitter grin.

He weighed the .45 in his hand and studied it thoughtfully. Suddenly he thrust it at Tragg. "Now how do you aim to get us out of here?"

"First thing," Tragg said, shoving the revolver into his holster, "we'll have to have horses. I figger our best chance is to make for Jessup's headquarters and borrow two of his. There was nobody there when I came by the place, except for a stove-up wrangler."

Morrasey thought about this for some time. At last he nodded. "It might do. It's a long walk, though, most of it across open prairie."

They were an hour from the creek, plodding up a gravelly slope, when they suddenly topped the rise and almost ran head on into the horsebacker. Tragg recognized him immediately as the dog handler, Jed Purdy. The five hounds, with their tails between their legs and great fat tears streaming from their sad eyes, trailed dejectedly behind Purdy's roan.

Purdy reined up sharply, staring wide-eyed. Almost immediately he began grabbing for his revolver. Tragg, with a sinking sensation in his gut, shouted an incoherent warning. The dogman could have been deaf, for all the attention he gave it. At what seemed the very last instant before Purdy would clear his .45 and kill them both, Tragg grabbed his own revolver from his holster and fired.

Purdy yelled in shocked amazement before there was time to start feeling pain. He stared in sick dismay as blood welled up on his forearm. His .45 clattered to the ground. Only then did Tragg allow himself to breathe.

"Set easy," Tragg told him, his voice surprisingly even and unruffled. The dogs sniffed and barked excitedly. Jed Purdy stared at Tragg and Morrasey. Until this moment Morrasey had merely stared blankly, paralyzed by the suddenness of the action. But now, from the corner of his eye, Tragg saw the sodbuster jerk the rifle to his shoulder.

Tragg, almost offhandedly, knocked the rifle down. Purdy, with blood now dripping from his fingertips, stared at them with growing panic. Tragg could sense what he was going to do. "Drop your reins," he said sharply, "and get down!"

Purdy spurred the roan viciously. The animal reared, startled. The dogman lurched in the saddle, only inches from the muzzle of Tragg's .45. I've got to stop him, Tragg told himself grimly. I can't let him go back and tell the others.

But he did not pull the trigger a second time. In the back of his mind he heard Morrasey snarling curses. Again the sodbuster jerked the rifle to his shoulder, and again Tragg knocked it down. In the meantime Purdy had hauled his roan down and was streaking back toward Dead Man's Creek.

Morrasey was raving shrilly, "You fool! Why didn't you kill him!"

"I think," Tragg said coldly, "we've had about all the killin' we need."

Abruptly Morrasey's mood seemed to change. He gazed at Tragg with a savage but icy amusement. "I'll bring that to mind when them cowhands catch us and string us up together."

They started back toward the creek. If they had to make a stand, better it was in a creek bottom than on open prairie. Time was the thing now. Time for tempers to cool. Their lives might well depend on time, if they could somehow buy enough of it.

At the moment it seemed an unlikely possibility. Purdy, on his roan, could easily reach his partners and bring them back before Tragg and Morrasey could reach the creek on foot. Still, there didn't seem to be much sense in standing still.

Morrasey, sensitive to the same urgency that Tragg was feeling, broke into a jog, and Tragg had to run to keep up with him. Soon they were gasping for breath, their lungs burning. After a time Morrasey fell into a weed patch and rolled on his back. Tragg fell beside him, gulping air.

We can't go on like this, Tragg told himself angrily. We'll never make it to the creek at all.

Morrasey was watching him closely. "You're the fancy lawman here. It's your job to see I live to stand trial, ain't it?"

"Yes," Tragg said warily, "it's my job."

"How do you aim to go about it? We ain't never goin' to make it to the creek. And we sure can't make much of a stand on open ground."

For the moment Tragg was too winded to talk, or even think. He lay staring into the bottomless depth of the sky. Why did I ever agree to take this job? he wondered.

Morrasey had just given him the answer. He was the lawman here. "If I am not a lawman," he said aloud, "I am nothing."

Morrasey looked at him doubtfully but made no comment. After a moment they forced themselves to their feet and started again toward the creek.

They jogged for what seemed a long time. "That dogman," Morrasey panted. "Most likely he's back at the shack by this time."

"Your place?"

The sodbuster grunted. "Fifteen minutes, I figger. Twenty at the most. That's what it'll take them to get here."

Tragg gazed with dismay at that distant green swath that marked Dead Man's Creek.

"I told you!" Morrasey said in a wheezing snarl. "You ought to of killed that dogman."

There were times, Tragg thought darkly, when killing seemed to be the only answer. It had been that way with Jody Barker. Even now, after all those years, Tragg could think of no other way that it could have ended. And it might be that Morrasey was right about Purdy. Somehow this uncertainty bothered Tragg more than the fact that they would soon be trapped on the open prairie.

Suddenly Morrasey grabbed Tragg's arm and gasped, "Look at that!"

The two men came to a rubber-legged halt and stood side by side on a grassy knoll, thoroughly vulnerable and defenseless, watching the buggy come toward them from the north.

"You make out the driver?" Morrasey asked between gulps of air.

". . . Not yet." Tragg watched closely with slitted eyes.

Morrasey made a sound of wonderment when he recognized the driver. "Ain't that the woman on the mud wagon?" He shot Tragg an ugly, yellow-tooth grin. "Seems that I recollect her takin' a shine to you. Them fancy duds, I guess. Well, that's all right with me. She might just save our hides for us, with that horse and buggy."

The light rig, with the top folded back and a gray mare between the shafts, rattled to a halt. For a moment Jessie Ross stared at Tragg with a faintly superior air. "I gathered," she said dryly, "from what I heard in town, that you left Bosen's Grove on the sheriff's horse, and with the sheriff's rifle in the saddle boot. Where are they now?"

Tragg made a weary gesture with one hand. "No time for that now. What are you doin' here?"

"To warn you about Callahan."

Tragg looked at her blankly. "Callahan?"

"Jody Barker's widow has hired him to kill you."

Tragg stared at her but was not overly surprised. Now it was clear why Rose Barker had insisted on working for her keep, although Tragg had banked the bounty money in her name and had, for ten years, sent her more than enough to live on. She had been saving her money to hire an assassin.

"How'd you know where to find me?" Tragg asked.

"I didn't know. But when I heard the shootin' I thought I better take a look." Her gaze narrowed. "Was that you?"

He briefly sketched the encounter with the dogman. She listened in silence. Then, with a dryness of tone that brought heat to Tragg's face, she said, "So you shot him in the arm, just enough to make him good and mad? And then you let him go for his pals?"

Morrasey's glance went from Tragg to Jessie Ross, but his interest was shallow and unfocused. "Ma'am," he told her, "you two can chew the rag later. Now get that buggy turned around and haul us back to Jessup's headquarters."

Jessie shook her head. "Wouldn't do you no good. There's a fresh bunch of cowhands up there gettin' ready to join up with the others."

"Where's Callahan now?" Tragg asked.

"I ain't sure . . ." Despite her dryness, she sounded worried. "I just come from headquarters—according to the old wrangler, a man that looked like Callahan come that way about an hour ago. The wrangler thinks he aimed to join the men with the dogs."

Tragg was just beginning to appreciate what she had done. If she hadn't gone to this trouble to warn him, Callahan could have walked up to him at any time and killed him without warning and without danger to himself. Tragg allowed a small smile. "Much oblige for tellin' me." He wanted to ask her why she had bothered, but time was running short. "I take it you don't advise goin' back to Jessup's headquarters and tryin' to catch some horses."

"Not unless you're anxious to get yourselves hung."

Tragg thought for a moment. Nothing had changed. They would still have to make for the creek.

"And then what?" she asked.

"If we hold out till dark, maybe tempers will cool. Maybe Ellender's regular deputy will show up in time to help."

Morrasey snorted impatiently. "That's enough jawin'. I'll feel safer when we get some timber around us."

Callahan joined the posse of cowhands after Jed Purdy returned from his encounter with Tragg and Morrasey. Bob Rayburn, the man who had been Omar Jessup's foreman, questioned him suspiciously.

Callahan was dimly amused at these hot-eyed, angry men. They took everything so emotionally. They were all burning to string Morrasey up to the nearest cottonwood, and within a matter of hours they would, every one of them, be regretting it bitterly. Emotion. Worst reason there was for killing a man.

But Callahan made himself sound as indignant and angry and as lustful for vengeance as the cowhands themselves. "Word's out at Bosen's Grove," he told them, "about the sodbuster killin' the cowman. Fellow name of Jessup. He a pal of yours?"

"He was our boss."

Callahan nodded in understanding. "I know how you feel. I'm a cowman myself, from up above the Cap Rock. I'd be proud to help you catch that sodbuster, if it's all the same with you and your friends."

They studied him for a moment. He could as easily be a

cowman as anything else. "Proud to have you with us," Bob Rayburn said with a quick nod.

One of the cowhands had slashed off Jed Purdy's sleeve and was using it to bind up the dogman's wounded arm. "I'll tell you the truth," Purdy said bitterly. "It's that duded-up deputy that I want to see hung. Just as much as Morrasey."

Callahan was instantly alert. "You mean Tragg?"

"I don't know his name. Got hisself done up like a Mex vaquero on his saint's day. Shot me, by God!"

The newcomer smiled to himself. This promised to be even easier than he had hoped. After the cowhands obligingly led him to Morrasey and Tragg, the rest would be simple.

CHAPTER NINE

As soon as they reached the wooded creek bottom Morrasey vaulted out of the buggy and tied the mare in a tangle of brush. Then he hurried back up to the slope to where Tragg and the girl were looking for the posse. The prairie was empty; there was no sign of Omar Jessup's self-appointed avengers.

"Where you reckon they are?" Morrasey asked.

Tragg shook his head. "I don't know, but I'm glad they're takin' their time. At least it'll give Miss Ross a chance to get away."

Morrasey looked at him in surprise. With so many things happening all at once, he hadn't had much time to think about the woman. He looked at her with a narrow, calculating gaze that sent a warning prickle over the surface of

Tragg's skin. "Well, now," Morrasey said, his yellow teeth flashing, "we haven't put the question to the little lady yet, have we? We don't even know if she *wants* to go."

Tragg scowled, thrown off for a moment by the devious paths of the sodbuster's reasoning. "Of course she wants . . ." Almost instantly he found himself looking into the muzzle of Morrasey's rifle.

"The woman stays with us," the sodbuster said flatly. "For a while, anyways. Until I get somethin' figgered out." He snarled at Jessie Ross, "Haul his handgun out of his holster and fling it over here to me. Slow and easy—or I shoot your man in the gut."

Jessie stared for a moment. Tragg said, "Don't listen to him . . ." But she waved his words off impatiently.

"He means it," she said. "I've seen his kind before."

Morrasey grinned. "Smart woman you got there, Deputy. Not hard-lookin' either." Jessie cautiously lifted Tragg's .45 out of the holster and flung it into the weeds. Morrasey picked it up and slipped it into his pocket. "Now," the sodbuster said, as the plan slowly took shape in his mind, "we'll just set here and wait for the cowmen to come. When they do, maybe then you'll get your pistol back."

Tragg felt a trickle of sweat go down his back. He was disgusted with himself for allowing Morrasey to disarm him a second time—still, he sensed that Jessie was right in her estimation of the sodbuster. Killing cowmen had become a deadly serious business to Morrasey, and he was quite capable of killing anyone who tried to interfere. "Morrasey," he said, sounding calm and reasonable, "don't you figger you're in enough trouble as things stand? It'll just put you in worse with the law if you hold Miss Ross here against her will."

Morrasey laughed tonelessly. "Can't be any worse, Deputy. Things're already as bad as they can get." He gestured impatiently. "Maybe I'll let her go later. I ain't got it all straight in my head yet."

"Morrasey," Tragg said coldly, "if you're thinkin' of usin' Miss Ross as a shield . . ."

"Shield?" Morrasey looked blank. The possibility had never crossed his mind. "No, sir," he said slowly, "that ain't what I was thinkin' about at all . . ." He turned, gazed to the south, and became suddenly alert. The three of them saw the feather of dust at the same time, and at the same time knew what it meant. Morrasey looked at them and sighed—but it was not a sigh of disappointment. "Well, there they are. Now we know why they took so long about gettin' here."

Apparently the wounded dogman had caused the hotheads to have some second thoughts. Instead of rushing in for a quick but risky kill, they were sealing the creek at either end, with the aim of methodically driving them into the open.

Morrasey gestured with the rifle. He knew now what he must do. "Up that way."

"What's up that way?" Jessie Ross asked.

"There's a dry wash that maybe them cowhands haven't thought about yet. If we get there before sundown there's just a chance we can slip out of this creek bottom without gettin' ourselves shot."

She didn't believe him, and neither did Tragg. Morrasey looked at them and suddenly sounded a burst of bone-grating laughter. "Not that it makes any difference." He turned to Tragg. "You'll do like I tell you. Or I'll kill the woman."

For the best of an hour, under the threat of Morrasey's rifle, they worked their way upstream through the heavy underbrush. Tragg went first; Morrasey was next, with the rifle touching Tragg's back; Jessie Ross came last, leading the mare. It was at Tragg's insistence that they had brought the mare, in the hope that Jessie would have a fair chance of getting away—if there really turned out to be an escape route, as Morrasey claimed. Surprisingly, Morrasey had made no strenuous objections.

It was almost sundown when Jessie tripped in a tangle of vines and fell sprawling. "I can't go any farther," she panted. "I've got to rest."

Morrasey looked at her coldly. "All right, we'll hold up a spell. No monkeyshines, Deputy, or I'll shoot her." He grinned unpleasantly, then moved up the bank and sat on a cottonwood log where he could watch them. Tragg knelt beside Jessie.

"You all right?"

She nodded. "Just a little winded." She lowered her voice. "What do you think?"

"Morrasey knows this country better than we do. If there's a way of gettin' out of here, he's the one that'll have to find it."

"Maybe. But I don't like the notion of puttin' my life in the hands of a lobo like him."

Tragg grinned wryly. "I'm not crazy about it, myself."

From his place on the cottonwood log, Morrasey stroked

his rifle and eyed them with suspicion. He was dull with exhaustion, and it took a real effort to keep himself from being drawn back into that misty world of the past.

Tragg sat in a stand of green mullein beside Jessie Ross. "There's somethin' I've been aimin' to ask you about," Jessie said. "Why you let that sheriff talk you into takin' this job anyhow? Not just to save *his* hide, I hope." She looked at Morrasey.

Tragg smiled wearily. "I don't know that I could tell you, if I tried. And I don't think I'll try." He turned to look at her. "Come to think of it, there's somethin' I've been wonderin' about. How'd you find out about Callahan?"

"I heard him talkin' to the Barker woman back at the boardinghouse. That's some woman," she said acidly. "Do lawmen make enemies like her every time they kill a man?"

"I don't know. Jody Barker was the only man I ever killed."

She looked incredulous. "All the years you was a deputy marshal and you never killed but one man?"

He smiled thinly. "Some lawmen never have to kill anybody at all." Fully aware that this conversation was leading them nowhere, Tragg shrugged his shoulders and hoped the matter would drop.

She pursed her mouth thoughtfully. "Coly Brown wasn't much more'n half your age when he'd killed four, five men in gunfights. Didn't you ever have a gunfight like that?"

"No. Not the way you mean."

"How did you kill Jody Barker?"

At first Tragg thought he would ignore the question. But

then, she had come all the way from Bosen's Grove to warn him about Callahan, so perhaps she had a right to an answer. "We was up in the Antelope Hills," he said, "shootin' at each other with rifles. It went on almost half a day, both of us dodgin' from one rock to another. In the end Jody got careless."

They sat for a while saying nothing. Then, almost against his will, Tragg broke the silence. "While we're clearin' the air, you never have said what made you go to all this trouble just to tell me about Callahan."

She brooded for a moment. "Because I hate Callahan, I guess. He's been a plague to me ever since we left Tascosa."

Both of them watched Morrasey, who crouched sullenly on the log, his eyes dull, his thoughts turned inward. "I talked to the sheriff about Coly," she said suddenly, for no apparent reason. "He's goin' to send word to the old Mex—Don Carlos Valona."

"No regrets about turnin' Coly in?"

"Why should I have any regrets?" she asked indignantly. "It was Coly's idea to begin with—I told you that."

Tragg seemed to sigh without actually doing so. "You'd of stood a better chance of collectin' the bounty if you hadn't taken it in your head to warn me about Callahan."

"You sorry I did it?"

He smiled faintly. "I guess not." Then, after a brief silence he said, "Coly Brown must of liked you pretty well."

Her eyes flashed. "He was crazy about me. He told me so all the time. Is there anything wrong in that?" Suddenly her expression became blank and cunning. "Didn't you ever feel that way about a woman?"

It occurred to Tragg that this was the most bizarre conversation that he had ever taken part in. Jessie's bluntness caused him to shift in discomfort. He could feel the heat of embarrassment in his face. More than embarrassment—anger, as well.

"Well," she persisted, "haven't you ever loved a woman?"

It was because of the anger that he turned to her and said, "I was married once."

She blinked. Somehow this was not the answer she had expected. "You're not married now?"

"My wife's . . . dead."

She looked at him and, for once, could think of nothing to say.

Morrasey watched the glowing coal of a sun settle on the horizon and told himself that they ought to be pushing on. Every minute they rested here lowered his chances of carrying out the plan which was now fully grown in his mind. The possemen would be scouring the creek bottom by this time, hoping to locate them before darkness fell—still, he couldn't seem to make himself move. He felt heavy and sluggish, and his gut ached with hunger. But he had known hunger so often that he had come almost to consider it a natural condition.

Lord, he thought bleakly, how many meals we missed, Delly and me! Hard times they were crying, all the way from the Platte to the Bravo—well, he and Delly could tell them all a thing or two about hard times.

Suddenly a terrible blackness washed over him. He

thought of Delly planted there along with all the other dead things in that sterile ground. A blackness of loss and despair that went right to the marrow of his bones. A blackness so terrible that everything else was blotted out. It was almost like being dead himself.

The heart-stopping plunge into the pit of depression lasted only a short time. A thing so awful could not be sustained for long. The unthinkable could not be thought about, except indirectly and for short periods.

He sat in a cold sweat, listening to the murmur of Tragg and the Ross woman talking, hearing them but not understanding or caring what they were saying. The blackness lifted and was replaced by a mood that was gray and deadly.

The death of Omar Jessup had been a disappointment to Morrasey. He knew now that he had expected the impossible—he had expected the killing of a single cowman to help ease his own sense of loss. But it hadn't really helped. How could the death of one cowman settle the score for Delly?

He knew now that it couldn't. He had had the innocent notion that, after Jessup was dead, he would simply pick up and go somewhere else and live his life more or less as before. But without Delly, of course. And that was the trouble.

He sighed and stared up at the sky which was slowly changing from blue to milky white to gun-metal gray. He felt limp and empty-gutted, the way a man feels when he comes out of a bad dream. The trouble was, Morrasey's world of reality wasn't much better than his dreams.

He slumped like a stone, watching the light drain from

the sky. He did not care one way or the other about the coming night, but he cast about anxiously for ways to hold back his own personal blackness. *What I ought to of done,* he told himself, *was kill every cowman that crossed my path. They all helped to kill Delly.*

Jessie Ross said, "The cowhands might decide to lay back for the night and flush us out in the morning. But if I know Callahan, he ain't the kind to set still and let a bunch of cowhands string you up, when the Barker woman *paid* him to kill you."

Tragg grunted, indicating that the same thought had occurred to him.

"What's the matter with *him?*" Jessie asked, shooting a look at Morrasey. "You think he's loco?"

"Men have always wondered about other men that kill in cold blood." For a moment Tragg recalled the terror-etched features of an Indian girl that Jody Barker had killed years ago, for no good reason that anyone ever discovered. Perhaps it had simply amused him to kill her, or perhaps he had seized on terror as a key to power—in those days Jody, with the help of a renegade band of Choctaws, had been running illegal liquor into the Territory.

Jessie was silent for a moment and then took another tack. "When," she asked bluntly, "did your wife die?"

Tragg didn't like this turn at all. "What do you mean?"

"Before or after you killed Jody Barker?"

He was offended by these personal questions. Still, Jessie Ross had gone to considerable trouble on his account. "Before," he said. "A little while before."

She cocked her head, thinking. "Where was she at the

time?" she asked. "I mean, where did she stay when you was off in Indian Territory ridin' for the marshal?"

"My wife," he said coolly, "was in Missouri at the time. With her folks."

"Visitin'?"

"Miss Ross," he asked stiffly, "would you tell me why you're askin' these questions?"

She cocked her head again in that birdlike way. "I was gettin' nosy," she admitted. "That's what come from livin' amongst men for so long. A woman needs other women to talk to now and again. Was that the trouble?"

"What?"

"Your wife. Is that the reason she went back to her folks?"

"That's not what I said."

She shrugged, disregarding the hostility in his voice. "It's what you meant. Didn't she like you bein' a lawman?"

She had guessed it so precisely that for a moment all he could do was stare. "I believe that's enough about my wife."

"Tragg . . ." Morrasey's nasal whine cut through the stillness like a saw. The sodbuster gestured with his rifle and Tragg went over to him. "Do you think there's a chance for me, if we get out of this? Could a sodbuster get a fair trial back at Bosen's Grove?"

Tragg thought about it, and that brief hesitation told Morrasey all he needed to know. The sodbuster laughed—a rasping sound totally without humor. "That's what I figgered."

"You'll get better treatment from the court than from

the cowhands."

Again Morrasey sounded his rasping laugh. "That ain't sayin' much." He bit off some tobacco and chewed for a while in silence. "Looks like things kind of got switched around, don't it, Deputy? You come lookin' for me to take me to jail, and now it looks like Frank Morrasey'll have to save your hide for you."

"Do you really know of a way out of here?"

"Maybe . . ." Tragg saw the flash of yellow teeth as Morrasey grinned. Then, with his old sullenness, he shoved Tragg away with the muzzle of his rifle. "You and your woman get your jawin' done. Pretty soon we'll be startin' upstream again. And Tragg . . ."

Tragg looked back.

"No monkeyshines. Or I shoot her."

"What did he want?" Jessie asked when Tragg returned, and for the first time she sounded frightened.

"He's workin' somethin' out in his head."

"Is he finished?"

"I think so."

Callahan and one of the new bunch of cowhands were hunkered down beside a fire drinking coffee. The cowhand, known to Callahan as Arkansas, snapped his dead smoke into the night and drawled, "She ain't much of a whingding, when you get right down to it. The sodbuster settin' down there on the creek bank, and us settin' up here, just waitin' for daylight to finish him off. I was kind of hopin' for more fun."

"There'll be fun enough," Callahan said dryly, "come daylight."

"You don't reckon he can get away from us, do you?"

"How could he get away? There must be more'n a dozen of us, and there's just one of him. Unless you want to count that fancy-rigged deputy."

Arkansas grinned at the fire. "And the woman. Don't forget her. Not a hard looker, accordin' to Jessup's wrangler."

Callahan went to see about his horse. That fool woman! he thought in cold fury as he pretended to reset his saddle. He never would have hired out to kill Tragg if he had guessed that Jessie Ross would take it in her head to interfere. The mood these cowhands were in, she was in a good way of getting herself killed along with the sodbuster and Tragg.

Except for the bounty, Callahan could have killed her himself. The trouble she was putting him to. The risks she was forcing him to take. Except for her, he could have simply walked up to Tragg, smiling disarmingly, and shot him dead. It could have been as simple as that.

But not any more. Tragg had been warned, thanks to Miss Jessie Ross.

He took his horse off the picket rope and walked the animal back to the fire where Bob Rayburn was helping himself to the coffee. "How's it look?" Callahan asked.

The foreman shrugged. "They're bottled up in the creek bottom. I've put men to ridin' the creek, just to make sure they don't get out. Come daylight we'll finish it off."

"Anybody seen any sign of them?"

"Turkey Bledsoe thinks he heard somethin' upstream, close to that stand of cottonwood. Not that it makes any difference. We'll haze them out when the time comes."

Callahan glanced up at the small white moon. "Too hot to sleep," he said. "I think I'll ride upstream and spell one of the guards."

As Callahan rode away from the fire another problem occurred to him. Rose Barker had not struck him as being a particularly generous woman. No, he thought grimly, a woman like that would demand full service for her money. If the cowhands, instead of Callahan, killed Tragg, Callahan might as well forget about collecting the balance of the money.

This was just another reason why he had to reach Tragg ahead of the posse. And this, he now realized, might be a full night's work.

A dark figure materialized against the darker background of the brush. The rider shouted a challenge. Callahan identified himself, recognizing the red-faced cowhand known as Turkey Bledsoe.

"Anything goin' up here?"

"Quiet as a graveyard." Turkey laughed.

"I guess," Callahan said pleasantly. "But I was just talkin' to Bob Rayburn. He says you heard the sodbuster and his pals rattlin' around down there by some cotton-woods."

Turkey scratched his heavy jaw. "Well, I heard some-thin'. It *might* of been them. How many of the boys you figger we've got down there?"

"Somebody said two dozen or more."

The cowhand's voice turned hard. "Good. More the better, I say. Does a man good to see a sodbuster hang now and again. You didn't know Omar Jessup, did you?"

Callahan admitted that he had never had the honor. Turkey

turned his head and spat savagely at the ground. "He was a good cowman and a first-class boss. I wouldn't want to be in that sodbuster's shoes. Nor the deputy's either."

"I guess," Callahan said noncommittally. After a moment he asked, "Where was it that you think you heard them?"

Turkey pointed at a dark shape directly behind him. "By that big cottonwood."

They looked at the dark tree. Callahan said, "I'll be glad to spell you. Why don't you ride back to the fire and get some coffee?"

Callahan watched the rider move off, slowly blending against the dark brush and finally disappearing completely. He dismounted and tied his own animal in a thicket of mesquite. Cautiously, he moved downstream from the cottonwood until he was well into the undergrowth. Then he cut back toward the tree, and that was when he almost tripped over the buggy shafts. "Well, now," Callahan thought aloud with stolid satisfaction, "they've got the horse with them. They can't do much travelin' in this brush without makin' considerable noise . . ."

The trio had been moving cautiously upstream for only a few minutes when Jessie Ross lost her footing and crashed through weeds and brush to the very edge of the water. She shrieked involuntarily as she went over the bank, and it seemed to Tragg that the sound must have been heard all the way to Tascosa.

"Get me out of here!" Jessie wailed, clawing at the clay bank.

"Shut your mouth!" Morrasey snarled, and his tone was

so savage that she was immediately silent. For several minutes they stood like Indian totems, hardly daring to breathe. At last Tragg turned to Morrasey. "You hear anything?"

"... I guess not." But he didn't seem sure, and they held their rigid positions for another full minute before Tragg knelt and held his hand down to Jessie Ross. When he had pulled her up over the lip of the bank, he asked, "Are you hurt?"

"I don't think so. Just scratches." Suddenly she shuddered. "And scared. I couldn't see the bottom when I began to fall. I couldn't tell how far down it was."

"How much farther are we goin'?" Tragg asked Morrasey.

The sodbuster's tone was predictably ugly. "Not far. If you can keep your woman quiet for a while."

Tragg was on the verge of hotly denying ownership to Jessie Ross or any other woman, then he realized that a quarrel at this time would be foolish and possibly fatal. "All right," he said with forced calm, "I think we're ready now."

From time to time they glimpsed horsebackers through the brush. To Tragg it didn't seem possible that any of them would be able to leave that creek bottom unseen, but Morrasey seemed to be growing more confident all the time. At regular intervals the sodbuster would stop and listen intently while peering into blank space. Then he would go on at a cautious pace, muttering to himself.

"Hold up!" Morrasey hissed suddenly. He stopped so abruptly that Jessie Ross piled into him and Tragg stumbled and almost fell beneath the hoofs of the mare.

Now they could see the horsebacker coming toward them, picking his way through the brush. "He's seen us," Morrasey snarled under his breath. "Or heard us, anyway. Well, there ain't nothin' for it now." He raised his rifle to his shoulder.

Tragg lunged forward and grabbed the barrel before he could fire. "Do you want to bring the whole posse down on us?"

"They'll be on us anyway," the sodbuster shrugged, "soon's this cowhand gets close enough to see us."

"Just the same . . ." After several hours of being puzzled by Morrasey's attitude, which seemed to alternate between blind savagery and indifference, Tragg was at last reaching a conclusion about the man—and he did not find it comforting. Apparently the sodbuster had no particular fear of the posse, because he had already written himself off as dead. The chances of his being caught and hung by the first light of morning were almost overwhelming. And even if he did bring off an escape of some kind, he still had a cow-country trial and legal hanging to look forward to. It almost seemed that Morrasey had lost interest in living.

But not in killing. He was quite prepared to kill the approaching cowhand, even if it meant bringing the entire posse down on them. Before he could do it, Tragg jerked off his hat and flogged the mare across the rump.

The startled animal reared, then wheeled and plunged downstream. The cowhand, his attention following the sound, shouted, "They're gettin' away! Somebody stop them!"

The cowhand put spurs to his own horse and followed the noise. Soon others had joined him, and the creek bottom echoed with curses as they floundered in the heavy undergrowth.

Morrasey turned on Tragg, grinning viciously. "There went the only chance your woman had of gettin' away from here."

Tragg stared at him. "I'm beginnin' to think that Miss Ross never had a chance in the first place."

Morrasey chuckled softly. "It all depends, I guess. On how hard you want to fight for her."

"What's he talkin' about?" Jessie Ross demanded, her voice going shrill. "He said he knew a way to get us out of here!"

"I think he was lyin'," Tragg said with more calm than he felt.

"Why'd he do a thing like that? It's *his* hide the posse's after."

"I don't think Morrasey much cares about hisself," Tragg said, looking at the sodbuster. "He figgers the game's about up, any way you look at it. All that's left, the way he sees it, is kill as many of the possemen as he can, before they kill him."

Jessie Ross stared at Morrasey. "Is that right?"

"Mostly," the sodbuster confessed. He listened to the noise and confusion as the cowhands continued to beat the dark brush in their search for the mare.

Then, from out of nowhere, a cold breeze seemed to flow across Tragg's face. An instinct that not even ten years of acting the fool could deaden, drove him to abrupt action. He threw himself at Jessie Ross. The two of them crashed into the brush as the muzzle flash of a rifle lighted the creek bottom.

CHAPTER TEN

T HEY heard the bullet ripping through the weeds. The shot seemed to have paralyzed Morrasey; he stood wonderingly, muttering to himself, a gangling, slope-shouldered figure clearly defined against the dark background of mullein.

Tragg was tensed, expecting another shot to follow on top of the first. Jessie Ross, frightened and angered, was fighting to get to her knees. Tragg threw himself at her again and held her down.

Tragg snarled at Morrasey, "Get down, you fool!" But the sodbuster was still trying to grasp the meaning of what had happened. He glared at the deputy and stood erect, making an even bigger target of himself.

Tragg groaned. In his mind, Morrasey was as good as dead. Any moment now a second shot would bring him down.

Now Tragg knew why he had accepted the badge from Ellender. All these years he had set himself up as a lawman—now, one way or another, he had to find out if he was fit for the job.

Surprisingly, the shot that would have finished Morrasey never came. They heard the rifleman scuttling back into the brush. Downstream somewhere the posse pulled up short. The sudden silence was tense, expectant.

"Red," somebody called, "did you see anything?"

"A flash upstream, I think."

There was a confusion of noise as some of the possemen began reversing their direction in the brush.

Jessie was squirming again, trying to get to her feet. "Tragg, can you see anything?"

"Not much. But it won't take the cowhands long to run us down, if we don't start movin'. Morrasey . . ." He shot a look at the sodbuster. "You all right?"

Morrasey laughed abruptly, and the sound was as unpleasant as ever. For a moment they were silent. Then Jessie Ross said in a puzzled tone, "I don't understand why that posseman didn't finish him off when he had the chance."

"I don't think it was a posseman." Tragg pulled her to her feet. "It must have been Callahan hopin' to earn his scalp money quick and easy, before the posse got to us."

Jessie still didn't understand, and Tragg said, "I guess he was afraid to shoot at me again, afraid of hittin' you. Without you, he couldn't collect his part of the bounty."

"The bounty," she said, comprehension coming slowly. "That would be Callahan, all right. He sure wouldn't want to go and kill me before I got a chance to collect."

Morrasey growled. "Hold tight to your woman, Deputy. The goin' won't be too smooth." He turned and disappeared into a tangle of vines.

They kept moving for what must have been the best part of an hour, slanting along narrow animal trails near the water, beating through the tall weeds higher up on the bank. At last Jessie fell to the ground, gasping.

Tragg himself was exhausted and would have welcomed a few minutes to get his breath, but Morrasey was hardly even winded. He looked back at them, sneering. "Got to keep goin' if you want to stay ahead of the posse."

With Tragg's help, Jessie pulled herself to her feet. "Now

. . . how much farther?"

"Not far now." Morrasey wiped his glistening face on his sleeve. The three of them listened for a moment to the distant sounds downstream. "Sounds like them cowhands can't make up their minds which way they want to go," he said with dry amusement.

"Right now," Tragg said with equal dryness, "it ain't the cowhands I'm worried about." His thoughts, as well as the thoughts of Jessie Ross, had turned to Callahan.

They stumbled for several minutes through a heavy undergrowth of thornbush. "Hold up," Morrasey said, pulling up abruptly.

They were standing on the edge of a deep gully, some nameless tributary, bone-dry except in springtime, that fed into the larger stream which was Dead Man's Creek.

Off to the north they could see the glow of one of the posse's coffee fires, but they seemed to have lost the cowhands themselves for the moment. About Callahan, Tragg was not so sure.

Tragg indicated the gully with a nod. "Where does it go?"

"Off on the prairie," Morrasey said indifferently—and his tone did little to ease Tragg's rising sense of suspicion. "Off towards the stage road," the sodbuster added. "That's what you wanted, wasn't it?"

"Let's take a closer look."

Tragg took Jessie Ross's hand and let her down to the bottom of the arroyo. Then he let himself down, and Morrasey came last in a clatter of rocks and loose earth.

They began to move slowly between the steep banks of the wash. After several minutes Morrasey pulled up sharply. "You hear anything?"

Tragg sucked in his breath and listened but heard only a ringing silence. There between the high walls of the arroyo they had even lost the noise of the possemen. "What was it like?"

Morrasey shrugged. Tragg was impressed with the feeling that Morrasey had somehow, in his mind, removed himself from the area of danger. His interest seemed to be that of an idle bystander who was not himself directly involved. Jessie Ross, holding to Tragg's arm, glared at Morrasey.

"I don't hear anything. Tragg, I don't trust him."

Neither did Tragg, but he didn't say so. "How much farther?"

"Pretty soon now . . ." Listening to the faint night sounds, Morrasey cocked his head and closed his eyes in thought. Then, to Tragg's irritation, he smiled. "You and your woman just foller after me, Deputy. It won't be long now."

They did seem to be moving away from the creek, but this fact did little to quiet Tragg's suspicions.

"Morrasey."

The sodbuster came to a shambling halt.

"I want to get up there," Tragg said, indicating the top of the bank, "and have a look around before goin' any farther."

Morrasey moved his bony shoulders in the barest hint of a shrug. "If you want to waste the time, it's all right with me."

Jessie was again grasping worriedly at Tragg's arm. "That sodbuster's leadin' us into a trap."

"I'll just take a look," Tragg said with as much patience as he could manage. He grabbed the twisted root of a salt cedar and pulled himself up until he could see over the grassy rim of the wash. He turned and stared out on that bald spread of gravel and grass that stretched off into darkness. What he saw put a knot in his gut but did not surprise him. The arroyo came to an abrupt end a little more than fifty yards ahead, at what appeared to be a shelf of sandstone.

In the milky light of a small moon Tragg could see the network of gullies and ditches focusing on that shelf of rock. It was easy to imagine the spring torrents rushing over the shelf and over the years, washing this arroyo out of the tough prairie. In the opposite direction he could see the dark swath of Dead Man's Creek and the fires of the possemen.

Then, as he gazed back along that twisting gully, he was seized by a sense of hopelessness. Jessie had been right about Morrasey—he had led them into a trap.

Later, when Tragg tried to recall all the details of the incident, he imagined that he had glimpsed the shadow flitting across the opposite wall of the arroyo, some distance down from where he had scaled the bank. Maybe he actually saw it and had already started to jump. All he was actually sure of was Jessie Ross shouting "Tragg!" A voice as taut as a bowstring.

He let go of the bank and started falling. The rifle boomed between those steep clay walls. He felt the slashing of the bullet beside his head. It seemed to Tragg that he was falling with nightmare slowness, like sinking in quicksand, and it seemed unthinkable that the rifleman

156

would not fire again and again, until finally a bullet found its mark.

Instead, Tragg found himself on the floor of the arroyo, rolling helplessly. In the back of his mind he heard the clatter of boot heels on the hard clay. The rifleman was rushing forward now, eager to finish the job.

That, Tragg thought with curious detachment, meant that the rifleman was not a posseman. There would have been more than one. It had to be Callahan.

Before Tragg had time to gather his senses—before he had even stopped rolling—he glimpsed Callahan's dark figure at the end of the arroyo. Callahan, cool and deadly, unruffled at having missed with his first shot, was now within easy range for his saddle gun. He dropped to one knee and brought his rifle unhurriedly to his shoulder.

Once, as Tragg rattled across the gravelly floor of the arroyo, he glimpsed Morrasey. The sodbuster was looking down at him, smiling coldly, his face a gray, disinterested mask in that pale light.

Tragg came to a jolting stop against the clay bank. Callahan smiled before he fired. Tragg could not actually see his face that clearly, but somehow he knew that Callahan was smiling.

A fatalistic chill dug its claws in Tragg's guts. Without a gun, there was nothing he could do. There was nowhere to run to, except to the bend at the upper end of the arroyo, and that was much too far away. Morrasey was already scuttling away in the shadows, making for that protective bend. Tragg could only stare into the muzzle of Callahan's rifle and wait.

A bleak, cheerless thought streaked across Tragg's mind.

Was this the way Jody Barker had felt when he knew that he was about to die? With the talons of panic in his guts?

A slight, quick figure darted in front of Tragg and threw itself at the rifleman. It took Tragg a moment to realize that the figure was Jessie Ross. He tried to shout a warning, and discovered that the breath had been knocked out of him in the fall.

A piece of clay wall disintegrated near Tragg's head. The sound of Callahan's rifle, channeled now between the close banks, was deafening. The bullet itself went screaming down the length of the arroyo and slammed into the intruding bank where the gully made its bend.

By this time Jessie was clawing at Callahan like a she-puma. Callahan knocked her away with a savage swipe of his hand. Supremely confident, he brought his rifle to his shoulder, only to have Jessie rush at him again.

This time Callahan took no half measures. He met her attack with the solid stock of his rifle. Something in Tragg's stomach knotted when he heard the violent sound of burled walnut against the side of Jessie Ross's head.

This brief, violent, and pointless scene had lasted only a moment. Jessie lay at Callahan's feet.

Callahan stepped into a swatch of pale moonlight. He grinned with cool amusement at the look of outrage on Tragg's face. His rifle held loosely, halfway to his shoulder, the big man casually planted his feet, setting himself for the rush that he was sure was coming.

The machinery of Tragg's mind ground to a stop. The scene and the actors in it seemed—for a moment—to freeze, and Tragg could see his position with painful clarity. He could give way to rage and charge Callahan—

and be quickly killed for his pains. Or he could turn and run; perhaps he could even make it to the temporary safety of the bend. In the meantime, what happened to the girl?

In Callahan's mind there was no question about what Tragg would do. He would fight. Not even in Callahan's world did a man stand by and do nothing while a woman was being clubbed to the ground.

Tragg took a quick, deep breath—then turned and ran.

Callahan was startled. Never would he have believed that the deputy would not, in the name of honor, obligingly rush in to be killed. He could not believe that a man of Tragg's old-world ways would run.

Nevertheless, Tragg ran. As Callahan, stolid and deadly, was raising his rifle to his shoulder, Tragg lunged to the dark side of the arroyo and made for the safety of the bend. The bounty hunter, who prided himself on being a sure judge of men, stared in disbelief. By the time he took himself in hand, Tragg was around the bend and out of sight.

Tragg sagged against the clay bank, gulping air. Morrasey regarded him with fascination. It was not often that Morrasey found someone he could feel superior to, but he now felt superior to Tragg.

He spat out his cud of tobacco and laughed. "Looks like I had you figgered wrong, Deputy. Anybody that turns his woman over to a lobo like Callahan can't be much account." Then he shrugged philosophically. "But it don't make any difference. Even a coyote'll fight like a she-bear when you get him cornered."

Tragg stared at him, still breathing with difficulty. "This arroyo is a trap," he said. "I know why you came here yourself. But tell me why you brought Miss Ross."

Morrasey chuckled, an abrasive sound in Tragg's ears. "I already told you, Deputy. Even a coyote fights when he's cornered. Course, I had one thing figgered wrong—I figgered you'd fight even harder, with your woman next to you. How come you run off and left her the way you did?"

"She's safe enough with Callahan. I couldn't see much sense gettin' myself killed for nothin'."

Morrasey grunted, admiring the logic but regretting the act. "I wouldn't trust that Callahan no farther'n I'd trust a cottonmouth snake. What's he got against you anyhow?"

"Nothin' personal," Tragg said dryly. "Somebody's payin' him to kill me."

Morrasey did not seem surprised. "Figgered it was somethin' like that. It's goin' to make things some harder."

"What do you mean?"

"Callahan. You'll have to do like he tells you, or he'll kill the woman."

Tragg shook his head. "He won't do that. The girl's worth a lot of money to him alive. She's not worth a thing to him dead."

Not even this seemed to surprise Morrasey. He gave a noncommittal grunt and listened to the excited, far-away voices of the cowhands. "Pretty soon they'll get tired chasin' their tails and somebody'll find this arroyo. Best we start movin'."

"No matter what way you go," Tragg told him, "this arroyo's goin' to turn out to be a deathtrap."

Morrasey flashed his yellow grin. "You foller me, Deputy. Might be there's some things about deathtraps that you ain't heard about."

Tragg allowed himself to be hazed quietly up the sandy bottom of the wash until they came to the dead end of the arroyo. There a sandstone shelf reached out over the gully like a huge drooping lid over a blind eye. The area directly beneath the shelf was partially blocked by a sandstone boulder.

Tragg dropped to one knee behind the boulder and saw that they had perfect field of fire straight down the arroyo for perhaps thirty yards. The rock shelf afforded protection from the rear and above.

"What do you think?" Morrasey asked with a tone of pride.

"We'll never get out of here alive."

Morrasey shrugged, as if living and dying were matters that no longer interested him. "Might be you're right. But if they want us, they'll have to come down in the gully to get us. A lot of cowhands'll get killed if they do that."

Now, Tragg knew, they were at the dark heart of the matter. Morrasey's single concern was in killing cowmen. He had brought Tragg with him in the hope that the deputy, in defending his prisoner, would kill yet more cowmen. That was the important thing. Nothing else mattered.

"Tragg!"

Callahan's voice rolled between the walls of the arroyo. Tragg was instantly alive in every pore. He looked sharply at Morrasey, and the sodbuster grinned.

"Tragg, you hear me?"

"I hear you."

"You know what my job is?"

"I know."

There was a brief silence. Morrasey regarded the deputy

with curiosity and amusement.

"I've got the girl, Tragg."

"I know that too."

There was another moment of humming silence. "Maybe I didn't make myself plain," Callahan said coldly. "I've got my pistol against Miss Ross's head. If you don't come out of that cave—or whatever it is—in one minute I'll kill her."

With an effort that made Tragg sweat, he kept his voice calm. "Don't be a fool, Callahan. Kill the girl and there'll be no bounty."

Callahan snorted. "There's a bounty enough on you. I'll be satisfied with that."

In his mind Tragg knew that Callahan was lying. Bounty hunters were greedy. They never had enough money. They were never satisfied.

But in Tragg's gut there was doubt. He wiped his sweaty forehead on his sleeve. Morrasey was still grinning and watching him like a toad watching an anthill.

"I figger half of that minute is already gone, Tragg. Thirty more seconds and I kill the woman."

Tragg tried to answer, but his mouth was dry and gritty.

Callahan sighed loudly in the darkness, a sound of resignation. Whether he was now resigned to killing Jessie Ross, Tragg couldn't tell.

"About twenty seconds left, Tragg."

Tragg looked at Morrasey and licked his dry lips. Morrasey chuckled at seeing the deputy squirm.

"Ten seconds, Tragg. You want me to kill her? It's up to you."

Sit easy, Tragg told himself. He won't kill her. There's no

sense to it. . . . But already he was on his feet and running in the pale moonlight.

Jessie Ross screamed in an eerily constricted voice as Tragg lunged from the light side of the arroyo to the dark. He heard Callahan's snarl of rage and guessed that Jessie had somehow, once again, managed to interfere with the bounty hunter's aim.

Callahan appeared suddenly, dark and threatening, around the bend. The muzzle flash seemed to flare in Tragg's face. The door to his mind slammed shut. He was in darkness and falling.

CHAPTER ELEVEN

H E was being dragged by his hands along the sandy bottom of the wash. Tragg worked his mouth in protest. His head was curiously numb. His vision was blurred.

The blurred vision, he noted with some relief, was caused by blood in his eyes. Then he must have a head wound, but not a bad one. Men with serious head wounds were not often in condition to worry about them.

Peevishly, he tried to pull away from the hands that were dragging him, but they tightened on his wrists and pulled all the harder. Slowly, like a very tired old machine beginning to turn, his brain began to function. As in a dream he saw himself dashing idiot-like from the protection of the rock shelf. Callahan had wasted one shot as Jessie Ross clawed at him, but apparently he had not wasted the second one.

Tragg felt himself being dragged behind the boulder and

dumped on a bed of gravel. He tried to ask a question, but he wasn't sure just what it was that he wanted to know.

Jessie Ross said angrily, "Shut up, until I get a look at you." Then, to Morrasey, "Move him over to the light. I've got to see how bad he's hurt."

Morrasey hunkered down and peered at the deputy's blood-smeared face. "Damn fool. I ought to of let that bounty hunter kill you. And I would have, except we might be needin' another gun hand before long." He lifted Tragg by the shoulders and moved him into a slant of moonlight.

Tragg watched the activity through a bloody haze. There was the sound of tearing cloth, and in a moment Jessie Ross had fashioned a compress and was binding it to his head.

Morrasey nodded approvingly. "You do that pretty good."

"I've had practice," she told him coldly. "Learning how to doctor bullet wounds was the first thing you had to do, if you wanted to be the woman of Coly Brown."

Now the numbness was beginning to leave him, and Tragg braced himself for what he knew was coming. He was not disappointed. Pain, brighter than an arrow, entered his head somewhere over his right ear. But with the pain there came also a certain order to his jumbled and disconnected thoughts.

"Callahan?" he asked.

Jessie Ross wiped the blood from his eyes.

"Callahan," she said, "is dead."

Tragg dwelt on this for a moment. It didn't seem possible that Callahan could be dead. "How?" he asked.

"Morrasey killed him. And a good thing for you he did.

Callahan was about to put another bullet in your head."

A sudden weariness pressed down on Tragg. He looked at Morrasey and said, "Why would you do a thing like that?"

"Maybe I like you." Morrasey grinned.

"No," Tragg said, thinking aloud. "You don't like anybody. Maybe you never have."

Morrasey drew back a bit, as if from the point of a knife. "That," he said icily, "is where you're wrong, Deputy. That's where you're dead wrong." He got to his feet and rested his rifle on the boulder and stood for a long while gazing out at the moonlit arroyo.

"Where," Tragg asked at last, "is Callahan now?"

Jessie shrugged. "Out there where Morrasey shot him."

"You and Morrasey will have to get the body out of sight. Cover it up, or drag it back here. The cowhands had accepted him as one of the possemen. If they find him dead . . ."

"I know," the girl said wearily. "The hotheads'll take charge of things if it looks like we've started killin' posse members. They'll shoot us out of this gully if it takes all summer. Do you think that hasn't crossed my mind?"

Tragg raised himself to his elbows, and the walls of the arroyo lurched sickeningly. "Then why didn't you get the body out of sight?"

"Morrasey wouldn't let me."

Suddenly Tragg felt older than his years. Morrasey was deliberately baiting the posse—if there had ever been a chance of talking reason to the cowhands, there was none now.

In a dry, impersonal voice, Jessie broke in on his

brooding. "That was a damn fool stunt, runnin' at Callahan the way you did. He wasn't goin' to hurt me—I thought you had sense enough to know that."

No one knew better than Tragg himself that he had acted the fool. When he looked at her he was surprised to see her smiling. Faintly, and a little grimly, but still smiling. "Thanks, anyhow," she said. "It's the first time a man ever throwed hisself in front of a gun on my account."

Then, somewhere in the night, a careless boot dislodged a small stone. It clattered down the clay bank to the bottom of the arroyo. Tragg knew that it was a waste of time, but he had to try once more to reach Morrasey.

"Morrasey, it's my job to see that you don't get strung up by a posse. I'll do the best I can. But you'll have to let Miss Ross go."

"No." Morrasey shook his head with finality. "It ain't that I've got anything against your woman, Deputy. But them cowhands wouldn't let her out of here anyway. I know cowmen. They killed Delly, didn't they?" He turned to stare out at the darkness. "Anyhow," he added harshly, "I need her here. I know how it's goin' to be in here, when the shootin' starts. Snappin' and snarlin' like a pack of hydrophobia coyotes, all of us. And the more of us there is under this shelf, Deputy, the more cowmen we kill."

Tragg stared at him. "What makes you think we won't turn on you?"

Another stone rattled to the bottom of the arroyo. Morrasey took a bite of tobacco and began to chew. "Like you said, it's your job to keep me alive. I figger that's just what you'll do, even if it means shootin' a few cowhands."

"No sense talkin' to him," Jessie said wearily. "He's got

his mind made up." Then in a quieter voice, "You still think it's worth the bother tryin' to get him back to Bosen's Grove alive? What difference does it make whether he dies here or on a hangin' scaffold?"

"Maybe it doesn't make any difference to Morrasey. It does to me."

She made a sound of exasperation. "I figgered you'd say somethin' like that." Then she smiled crookedly to herself. "It's funny, in a way. There's Callahan out there, dead as a stump. No bother to me, or anybody else. The whole bounty's mine. All I have to do is go back to Bosen's Grove and tell the old Mex where to find Coly. Funny."

Somewhere in the night a foot turned in soft sand. A nervous cowhand muttered an obscenity. Cautiously, Tragg started pushing himself to his feet, but Morrasey quickly shoved him down with the stock of his rifle. "I can't do you any good settin' here," Tragg told him.

"You'll do fine," Morrasey said flatly, "when the time comes."

"When will that be?"

Morrasey grinned stiffly. "When the bullets start snappin' around the little woman's head—that's when you'll do your part of the fightin', Deputy."

This was what it all boiled down to. This was the reason he had brought Jessie Ross with them and the reason he would not let her go. Morrasey had convinced himself that Jessie Ross was Tragg's woman, and nothing was likely to change his mind.

The sodbuster turned to Jessie and said thoughtfully, "I never got to know many women, except family. And Delly, of course. But I got to admit you're somethin' of a puzzle to me. What kind of woman are you anyhow?" As though he actually wanted to know. "Left your man back in Kansas. Figgerin' to sell his scalp to some old Mex in Bosen's Grove." He spat with disgust. "Oh, I know what you think about us folks that try to gouge a livin' out of the ground. Just sodbusters, you say. Not like people." Suddenly his voice was harsh with anger and frustration. "Let me tell you, we're just like anybody else. We hear things. We understand. We got feelin's."

Tragg felt the heat of unaccustomed shame rise in his face. He realized that Morrasey was right. These squatter farmers lived so near the edge of starvation that they no longer behaved or looked like ordinary people—it was easy to forget that they were people at all.

Jessie asked uneasily, "How'd you know about that bounty?"

"You talk about it enough." Morrasey flashed his ugly grin. "But you folks figger us sodbusters're like mules or fence posts. Don't hear much, and what we do hear we don't understand. Ma'am," he snarled with coarse irony, "it might surprise you some if you could see the things that went on inside our heads."

"I don't care what goes on inside your head," Jessie told him grimly. "Unless you've got notions about that bounty."

Morrasey looked at her with a bleak curiosity. "It ain't money I'm interested in."

"Then you're a fool."

Morrasey sighed. "There you go, never givin' us sodbusters credit for thinkin' a thing out for ourselves. I've got all the guns and you're my prisoners—how you figger that makes me a fool? And when the time comes, the deputy there is goin' to be fightin' and killin' cowhands, just like me. Not to save *my* hide. Not because it's his *job*. But because you're his woman." His eyes glittered. "He's already showed me once that he don't mind fightin', and even risk gettin' shot, on your account. I figger he'll do it again."

An oppressive silence bore down on Tragg and Jessie. "When it's all over," she asked wearily, "what good will it do? Even if some cowhands get killed? We'll all be dead."

Morrasey turned to Tragg. "That scare you, Deputy?"

"Some, I guess."

"Me too. Some." He seemed to be holding this fact to the light, examining it with a look of surprise. "Funny thing. Somehow I never counted on bein' scared."

"Let me talk to the possemen. Might be I can still get them to change their minds."

Morrasey shook his head. "I just said I was scared, not that I wanted them to change their minds."

Tragg became aware of Jessie Ross holding tight to his arm. He could hear the rustle of grass and the occasional grunt of a posseman as the cowhands closed in on the arroyo. It would be better, he thought, if they waited for daylight before attacking. Passions did not run as hot in daylight as they did in darkness. But he doubted they would wait.

It was still two hours before sunup when the possemen finished closing in on the shelf. Those who had come on horses had left their animals at the mouth of the wash. They were now spaced in the tawny grass on both banks.

Each rifleman focused his weapon on the dark gray boulder beneath the shelf, bringing the area into deadly cross fire.

Bob Rayburn was regarding the dead figure of Brian Callahan sprawled in the bottom of the arroyo. Red Gipson, the old Jessup hand, crawled up from Rayburn's rear and said, "Everybody's set. Waitin' for you to give the word."

Rayburn, a big, long-faced man who had been Omar Jessup's foreman for almost a dozen years, nodded to indicate that he had heard. "One of the boys found a rent buggy downstream," Red continued. "Guess it's the one the woman was drivin'. Looks like the three of them are still together. Morrasey, the dude deputy, and the woman." He thoughtfully scratched his lantern jaw. "All three of them was on that mud wagon that broke down."

"Four," Rayburn said tonelessly, "if you count the dead one." He sighed. "I wish the sheriff was here."

"Nothin' he could do. The boys have got their heads set on hangin' that sodbuster. Nothin' Max Ellender could say would stop them."

"Ain't the sodbuster I'm thinkin' about."

"The woman?"

Rayburn nodded. "None of us have done much thinkin' about what's apt to happen when this is over. Even if it was Morrasey by hisself, we'd be in bad with the law. The boys know that, don't they?"

"They know that Morrasey killed Omar Jessup. That's all they care about."

"Work your way back down the wash. Tell them to set tight while I try to get the woman out of there."

"All right," Red said doubtfully, "but some of them ain't goin' to like waitin'.""

Rayburn turned and looked at the red-faced Gipson. "Anybody that feels like takin' charge of this posse, tell him to come talk to me."

Rayburn turned his attention back to the wash while Red crawdadded back through the weeds. The foreman cupped his hands to his mouth and called toward the shelf, "Ma'am—whatever your name is—can you hear me?"

There was a stretch of humming silence. Morrasey's grating voice jarred the stillness. "She can hear you, Rayburn, but it don't do her no good."

There was not much hope in Rayburn's tone when he called, "Let her go, Morrasey. We've got no fuss with the woman. Ma'am, just walk out from under that shelf and straight down the wash. Nobody'll hurt you."

Morrasey laughed. "The woman stays with me and the deputy."

The foreman thought for a moment. "Let me talk to the deputy."

Morrasey grinned widely. This, from as far back as he could remember, was the first time a cowman had ever asked his permission for anything, and it amused him.

After a moment Tragg called, "You the leader of the posse?"

"Bob Rayburn. Omar Jessup's foreman. You're the one that Callahan told us about, I guess. The one that killed Jody Barker some years back. Well, if you outgunned Jody, you must know your business. . . . You must know that we can't let sodbusters get away with killin' cowmen."

"That's a job for the court, Rayburn."

The foreman sounded tired. "I don't aim to argue about it. We can shoot you out from under that shelf, or you can turn Morrasey over to us and save your own hide. It don't make any difference to us. But send the woman out. There's no sense gettin' her killed for nothin'."

Morrasey called in amusement, "It ain't for the deputy to say, Rayburn. He's been shot in the head and I've got the guns. If you want me, you'll have to kill all of us."

Rayburn turned over and looked at the sky. It was still more than an hour before sunup. "That the way it is, Tragg?"

"That's the way it is," Tragg said slowly, "now."

The foreman frowned. What did he mean by *now?* Was it a request for time? Did the deputy think the situation beneath the shelf would somehow change with the coming of daylight?

He directed his next question to the sodbuster. "Morrasey, I'm askin' you again. Let the woman go. She can't be any help to you."

"That's where you're wrong, Rayburn!" There was a wide grin in Morrasey's voice. "That's where you're dead wrong."

Red Gipson crawled along the lip of the wash and lay in the grass beside the foreman. "Some of the boys want to go on and get it over with. They're tired waitin'."

"Tired or not," Rayburn said grimly, "they'll go on waitin'. Until daylight, anyway."

"They won't like it. What's the sense of waitin' till daylight?"

The foreman made a vague gesture toward the shelf. "I ain't sure. What do you know about that deputy?"

"Just what Callahan told us. Duded up like a Mex vaquero at a Christmas *baile,* to hear him tell it. Took to the lecture platform and made a big thing out of killin' Jody Barker. You remember Jody?"

"I remember. And it wasn't no greenhorn that outgunned a lobo like Barker. I think he was tryin' to tell me somethin'."

"Tell you what?"

Rayburn sighed. "That's what I ain't sure about. Anyhow, I've made up my mind to let him have till daylight."

"The boys ain't goin' to like it."

The foreman turned to Red and said with a savagery that startled both of them, "The boys can go to hell!" Then, in a quieter voice, "Tell them we're holdin' off till sunup."

"Then what?"

"Then we get the sodbuster."

"Even if the woman gets in the way?"

"Yes." The foreman's wide mouth stretched in a mirthless smile. "It ain't like she's the *first* woman we ever killed."

Red looked at him worriedly. He had never heard Bob Rayburn talk like this before. Bob had been the maddest of the bunch when they first got word that Omar Jessup had been killed. But now, somehow, he was different. And Red wasn't at all sure that he liked the change.

After Red had gone, Rayburn lay staring down at the still body of Brian Callahan. As he viewed it he felt no sense of outrage or anger—Callahan had been a stranger. Still, it added to the mystery that had been building in the foreman's mind. They had known nothing about the man,

173

only what he had told them. Had he lied? Was it more than mere coincidence that a stranger—an uninvited member of the posse—should be the first one killed?

Many questions and few answers. What had started as a simple case of frontier justice had assumed a certain grotesqueness that the foreman found disturbing. There would be hell to pay if the woman was killed—still, they couldn't allow sodbusters to get away with murdering cowmen.

Morrasey was becoming more impatient as time went by. It had been almost an hour since they had last heard from any of the possemen. The sodbuster ventured out from behind the boulder and peered up at the top of the arroyo. Suddenly he shouted, "Why don't you do somethin', Rayburn? Your boys scared of a sodbuster?"

The sound of his voice rolled eerily between the walls of the gully. Morrasey ducked back under the shelf and hunkered down behind the boulder. There was no reaction from outside. "What're they waitin' on!" he snarled to himself. Then, in pent-up anger, he began pounding the stock of his rifle against the hard ground. "Goddamn them! Goddamn them!"

He slumped against the boulder and some of the rage went out of him. His mind flew back to other times and places. In his harsh, saw-edged voice he began humming the words of the old fiddling tune.

> Now up the rope I go, up I go;
> Yes, up the rope I go, up I go;
> And those bastards down below, they'll say,

"Sam, we told you so,"
They'll say, "Sam, we told you so,"
Goddamn their eyes!

Jessie Ross took Tragg's arm. "I wish he'd stop that racket. Whatever it is. You sure couldn't call it singin'." She squinted at the deputy. "How do you feel?"

"Better." The slashing pain in his head had settled down to an erratic pounding. "I've been thinkin'," he said quietly. "Might be I could keep Morrasey busy for a minute or so. Maybe long enough for you to make it down the arroyo to the bend."

"Thanks anyhow," she said dryly. "With the sodbuster shootin' at my back, and the cowhands shootin' at me from above, I'm better off here."

"They can shoot us out of here any time they feel like it. You know that, don't you?"

She shrugged. "Come daylight maybe they won't feel like it."

This was one hope that had lain in the back of Tragg's mind ever since he had come to in this deathtrap that Morrasey had selected so carefully.

"Course," Jessie went on in the same dry tone, "even if they don't change their minds, things maybe ain't as bad as they look. If they want to shoot us out of here, they'll have to come down in the wash. If they do that, somebody besides us is apt to get shot. Nothin' like seein' a pal on the ground with a bullet in his gut to take the spunk out of a mob. That's what Coly always said."

Morrasey was standing again, gazing intently around the side of the boulder. Tragg pushed himself to his feet. His legs were rubbery. His heart hammered. A shaft of pain seemed to pierce his skull above the right ear and embed itself between his shoulders.

Morrasey chuckled. "You ain't lookin' none too pert, Deputy. But you'll perk up when the shootin' starts."

Tragg peered out at the wash and for the first time fully appreciated the murderous field of fire that Morrasey had chosen. The cowhands, from their positions on the banks of the arroyo, might go on indefinitely smashing bullets against the boulder. But some hothead would soon get enough of that. He would climb down and attempt to rush their position and that would be the end of him.

Morrasey was looking at him, grinning. "See how it is, Deputy? It ain't all as one-sided as some of them cowhands might think."

Tragg closed his eyes. He knew now that he could not take Morrasey by surprise and overpower him. He knew that his play for time had gained them nothing.

"Set down," Morrasey told him. "Pretty soon now you'll be needin' your strength." He looked toward the wash and his tone turned thoughtful. "Recollect what I told you once, Deputy? About the way it's goin' to be? Like a pack of hydrophobia coyotes, snappin' and snarlin' and killin' everything that comes across our path. That's the way it's goin' to be here."

Tragg's legs began to quiver. He sat down.

"How much longer?" Jessie Ross asked quietly.

"First light in about half an hour."

"Is that what they're waitin' on?"

"The man called Rayburn's givin' us that long, I think, hopin' I can think of somethin' to stop the killin'. I can't.

And I don't think he'll be able to hold the cowhands much past first light."

"Coly used to say that lynch mobs are like bats—can't stand the light of day. Can't stand to look at one another, I guess. They'll want to get it over before the sun's too bright."

They sat in dull silence. The only sound was Morrasey shifting from one foot to the other, squinting over the barrel of his rifle.

CHAPTER TWELVE

ONCE again Red Gipson dropped into the grass beside Bob Rayburn. "I been talkin' to the boys. They ain't goin' to wait much longer."

Rayburn glanced up at the pewter-colored sky. Twenty minutes, he figured. Maybe half an hour before full light. Somewhere between sundown and first light the prospect of a hanging had gone sour. Somewhere along the line the foreman had allowed reason to dilute his anger. That was the trouble with being a foreman. You learned to think with your head instead of your guts.

"Want me to get them ready?" Red asked.

". . . Not yet. I've been doin' some thinkin'."

"Me too." Red grinned. "Thinkin' how that sodbuster's goin' to look swingin' on a cottonwood limb."

"Thinkin'," the foreman said with studied patience, "that maybe we're goin' off on the wrong track. Ellender *did* deputize that dude, and sent him to get the sodbuster. The sheriff ain't goin' to take it kindly, us lynchin' his prisoner."

Red didn't like the direction this conversation was taking. "Ellender's in town with a busted leg. Nothin' he can do about it."

"He won't always have a busted leg. I don't know about the rest of you, but I don't want to finish the rest of my days lookin' over my shoulder for Max Ellender."

Red thought about this. There was something about it that didn't ring true. And there was something about Rayburn, as well. "The boys ain't goin' to swaller that," he said, shaking his head. "Settin' here all night, stiff, cold, wet with dew. They ain't likely to be satisfied to just pick up and leave."

"I never said anything about pickin' up and leavin'. It just seems like there's better ways of goin' about this."

"What kind of ways?" the red-faced cowhand asked doubtfully.

"There's plenty Johnson grass down in the bottom, dry enough to burn, wet enough to make a good smoke. We could set it afire and push it off the shelf. That would bring them out in the open."

Red considered this in openmouthed concentration. "Might work. But what happens after we get them out of there?"

"One step at a time," Rayburn hedged. "First we get them out . . . then we'll see."

Red could see the way the foreman's mind was working, but it wasn't going to help the sodbuster. This was one thing that Red was sure of. Morrasey would hang—even if he had to turn the rest of the possemen against Rayburn.

Not much longer now, Morrasey thought to himself,

gazing out at the steely sky. Strange, in a way, how calm he was. He had expected it to be different. But the expectation of sudden violence had gone flat; even the acid bite of vengeance had gone slightly stale. He might have been one of those visiting play actors back at the opera house in Bosen's Grove, walking through a part, speaking the lines, from force of habit. Not even the prospect of more killing excited him—he'd just be glad to get it over with. He was tired. Maybe in the same way that Delly had been tired.

He realized that this was a passing dullness. There would be excitement enough later. And the bite of vengeance would be sharp and sweet, when it came. But all that would come later. At the moment his thoughts were out of focus, soft-edged and blurred.

Somewhere in his memory, a thousand miles away and a million years ago, a fiddle wailed. Clapping hands set a dragging tempo—it might almost be a funeral march. Thick-soled boots shuffled to half-heard music of an eerily minor key. Salute your partner. All join hands. Promenade. Ghostly dancers stomped and shuffled and curtsied and laughed. All in ghostly silence.

"Look at him," Jessie Ross said under her breath. "His mind's somewhere else, he's not thinkin' about us at all. Maybe I could get to the guns if . . ."

Tragg, who had been thinking along the same line, took her arm and forced her firmly back against the rock. There was movement now, and a gathering excitement, along the rim of the arroyo. Morrasey heard it and shot the two of them a quick glance. "Won't be long now, Deputy."

"I can't be any help without a gun."

"All in good time . . ." He held up a hand, scowling as

he listened. "What do they think they're doin' out there?" he asked of no one in particular. Cautiously, he peered around the edge of the boulder, half expecting a bullet beside his head. But the only sound was that of growing activity on the shelf above.

Then the familiar voice of Jessup's foreman called down. "Time's up, Morrasey. Send the woman out. You can have that much to your credit, anyways."

Morrasey grinned wolfishly and shouted an obscenity. Tragg motioned for Jessie Ross to stay where she was. He pushed himself to his feet. The effort left him panting.

Morrasey chuckled. "You'll feel better, Deputy, when the shootin' starts."

The first bundle of burning grass fell like an exploding star beside the boulder. The first strangling wisps of smoke drifted into their cavelike alcove. A spatter of rifle slugs smashed against the boulder.

Morrasey stared in bewilderment and rage. Another bundle of burning grass fell beside the first one. The smoke became thicker beneath the shelf. Jessie began to cough.

There was a wildness in Morrasey's eyes as he stared up at the edge of the shelf where the rain of fire was coming from. Tragg said with as much calm as he could muster, "They're not goin' to chance comin' down the wash, Morrasey. They don't have to. They'll just keep dropping that burnin' grass and pretty soon we'll have to come out for air."

Morrasey snarled like a badger in a steel trap. "I told them before, they'll have to come after me! And they will!"

Tragg shook his head. Now all three of them were coughing and their eyes were beginning to water. "Morrasey, let Miss Ross go."

Morrasey laughed bitterly. "Not much chance of that, Deputy. That woman of yours is my guarantee that you'll do your share of the fightin'." He moved to the far side of the boulder, staring through the smoke at the top of the wash. Suddenly he jerked the rifle up to his shoulder and fired. A cowhand on the lip of the wash yelled in pain.

Morrasey turned to Tragg, his eyes streaming. "Now you'll see, Deputy!"

From above there was, at first, a stunned silence punctuated by the groans of the wounded man. Then came the rush of anger, the harsh, threatening voices. Hotheaded Red Gipson, louder than any of the others, snarled, "I don't know about the rest of you, but I aim to kill myself a sodbuster!"

Rifle fire thundered between the banks of the wash. But the cowhands could see that their bullets were smashing harmlessly against the boulder. They soon got enough of that.

"Get yourself set, Deputy," Morrasey said with obvious pleasure. "The two of us together ought to kill a dozen of them cowhands before they shoot us out of here. Might even be"—he grinned—"that we can kill *all* of them, and Miss Ross'll come out safe after all."

Jessie got to her feet, coughing and wiping at her stinging eyes. "If I'm goin' to get shot anyhow," she said angrily, "I'd just as soon be on my feet."

Morrasey, who had been listening only to the sounds beyond the shelf, suddenly raised his rifle and fired into the smoke. Another storm of bullets assaulted the boulder. Then there was sporadic fire, just enough to make them keep their heads down while possemen lowered themselves into the wash.

Tragg, with pounding head and stinging eyes, turned to Morrasey and said, "Don't you think it's about time I had a gun?"

"Pretty soon now. They're comin' down into the wash." He flashed his yellow teeth and began to cough. That was when Tragg hit him.

The attack came as unexpectedly to Tragg as it did to Morrasey. Tragg grabbed the barrel of the sodbuster's rifle and clung to it with the stubbornness of a dog with a bone. Morrasey snarled and fell back against the dirt bank. Both men fell to the ground, still fighting for the rifle. Tragg lost his bandage and a warm wetness blinded him. Then, suddenly and mysteriously, Morrasey went limp.

Wiping the blood from his eyes, Tragg snatched the rifle and backed away. It was then that he saw Jessie Ross standing in the swirling smoke, holding a short-barreled saddle rifle in both hands, as if it were a club. Somehow she had managed to get around behind the two men and had grabbed one of the sodbuster's guns.

Tragg sagged against the boulder, panting. "Much oblige," he said dryly. "Thankin' you for savin' my life is gettin' to be a regular thing with me."

She fell into a fit of coughing and dropped the saddle gun. Tragg could hear the possemen sliding down the clay walls into the arroyo. His head throbbed. Smoke tears plowed muddy furrows into his beard.

More bullets poured in over the boulder and slammed

into the clay bank. There was confusion and angry shouting on the other side of the boulder. Green soldiers, Tragg thought, nerving themselves for an attack.

More bullets slammed through the opening. Tragg thought, "I can still make a deal with them about the woman." Morrasey, lying like a log at his feet, was no problem now. Then a dozen rifles seemed to fire at once. In the stunning silence that followed, a posseman plunged into the smothering curtain of smoke.

"Sodbuster!" The voice was shrill with rage. The posseman fired blindly and the bullet plowed into the ground at Jessie's feet.

Something inside Tragg went cold. As the cowhand, suddenly blinded by the smoke, fired wildly, Tragg lifted Morrasey's rifle and lashed at the dimly seen head. The walnut stock splintered. Tragg felt the shock all the way to his shoulders. The cowhand dropped without a word.

Tragg fell back against the boulder to get his breath. "You all right?" he asked the girl.

"Nothin' wrong with me," she said in a choked voice, "that some fresh air wouldn't cure."

Tragg turned to the arroyo and shouted, "Rayburn, the woman's comin' out. Hold your fire."

After a moment Rayburn's calm voice asked, "What happened to Red?"

"He's all right—for now," Tragg shouted back.

The foreman's voice turned cold. "What do you mean, Deputy?"

"I want your word that the woman'll be safe. Then maybe your pal will come out of this with nothin' worse than a sore head."

There was angry muttering in the wash, then silence. "All right," Rayburn called. "Morrasey's the one we want, not the woman."

Tragg stepped back and motioned for Jessie to move outside. "What about you?" she asked.

Tragg managed a faint smile and nodded at the stunned cowhand. "That depends on how many pals Red's got out there."

"You can give them the sodbuster . . ." She cocked her head and seemed to be listening for something. "Daylight now. They're not as worked up as they was last night. Turn Morrasey over to them and they'll let you go." When she saw that her speech was doing no good, she shrugged and asked, "Anything you want me to say to them?"

"Tell them," he said evenly, "I'm takin' the prisoner back to Bosen's Grove."

"They won't stand for it."

Tragg took her arm and shoved her toward the opening. She looked back at him, shook her head resignedly, then disappeared around the side of the boulder.

Tragg saved one .45 and unloaded the other weapons that Morrasey had collected. He nudged the sodbuster with the muzzle and said, "Morrasey, you hear me?"

The sodbuster groaned.

"We're goin' back to Bosen's Grove, Morrasey."

Morrasey looked up at him, his eyes swimming with hatred. Tragg moved over to the fallen Red Gipson who was now beginning to stir.

"There's something I want you to get straight," Tragg told him in the controlled voice of an experienced lecturer. "I'm takin' my prisoner to Bosen's Grove. Do you hear what I'm tellin' you?"

Red stared at him, dazed and angry. Tragg went on in the same even tone. "In just a minute we're goin' to leave this place. First the sodbuster, then you, and then me. If one of your pals decides he just has to shoot Morrasey when he comes out, I'll kill you."

Red Gipson stared. "You're loco!"

There was a faraway look in Tragg's eyes. "You may be right. But that won't make you any less dead if your pals shoot Morrasey."

Red crawled shakily to his hand and knees. "If you kill me, that bunch will shoot you to pieces."

The deputy smiled in a disturbing sort of way. "I believe you. But we're still goin' out of here the way I said. You want to talk to them before we start?"

The cowhand swallowed with difficulty. Nothing he said seemed to make the slightest impression on this ridiculous figure of a lawman. With Tragg's help, he pulled himself to his feet. Resting against the boulder, the cowhand spoke to the men outside.

". . . Bob. Can you hear me out there?"

There was a moment of expectant shuffling in the arroyo. Then Bob Rayburn's calm voice said, "We hear you, Red."

"Listen . . ." There was a tautness in Red's voice that caused his friends to freeze. "Listen, all of you, and listen good!"

In as convincing a way as possible, he told them what they must do.

They walked into the dry wash bristling with rifles. Morrasey first, then Gipson, and then Tragg, with the muzzle of his .45 pressed firmly against the cowhand's back.

There was at first an angry muttering. Someone—perhaps unconsciously—jacked a cartridge into the chamber of his weapon. "That's enough!" Bob Rayburn snapped.

The strange procession marched doggedly between the twin files of riflemen. Jessie Ross, who was standing at the far end of the wash, out of the line of fire, watched in fascination as they came toward her. Morrasey, it seemed, was caught in the grip of a paralyzing rage. Red Gipson was wild-eyed and sweating freely and looked as if he might be sick. Owen Tragg looked only grimly determined.

When they neared the bend in the arroyo Jessie Ross started toward them, but Tragg waved her to one side. "Have you seen any of their horses?"

She nodded. "On a picket rope down at the far end of the wash."

The deputy's face showed his relief. "We might get away from here yet—if Red's pals don't decide they'd rather see me dead than him alive."

When they reached the horses, Tragg looked bleakly at Red Gipson. "Set down over there with your back against the bank."

Red tried to sneer. But his heart wasn't in it. His head was bleeding. His guts were twisted with anxiety. There was a certain something about the lawman's tone that discouraged the thought of rebellion. He sat with his back against the wall of clay, watching as Tragg and the girl selected three animals for themselves and flogged the others toward the mouth of the wash.

Red had about convinced himself that it wasn't so important, after all, that they hang the sodbuster. Still, there was a front to be kept up, his face to be saved, even at some risk to his life.

"Even if you get that sodbuster to Bosen's Grove, the boys'll bust the jail down and get him."

Tragg didn't even bother to look at him. "That'll be Sheriff Ellender's problem." He quickly unbitted one of the animals and threw on a lead rope. "In the saddle," he snapped to Morrasey.

Morrasey looked at him dully. There was no way for Tragg to guess what went on inside the sodbuster's head, so he dealt with him cautiously, as he would have dealt with a shedding snake. "In the saddle," he said again, quietly—almost gently.

Surprisingly, Morrasey grasped the saddle horn and pulled himself up, almost wrenching the rig from the animal's back—the natural act of a man who was used to riding bareback mules, when he rode at all, and had never owned a saddle of his own.

"You all right?" Tragg asked. The words sounded foolish in his own ears, considering all the trouble the sodbuster had put him to. Morrasey looked down at him and nodded. All the fight seemed to have gone out of him. Once they had passed the gauntlet of rifles, his sense of rage seemed to burn down and die.

Jessie watched the scene with growing anxiety. "Hadn't we better think about gettin' away from here?"

They left Red Gipson sitting in the bottom of the arroyo. Jessie Ross, riding astride like a man, led the way on a spirited bay mare. Tragg came next, with Morrasey's animal bringing up the rear on a rope. They moved quickly to the end of the wash, and no one spoke until they had put Dead Man's Creek and its protective timber between them and the horseless possemen.

Jessie reined her mare down and fell in alongside Tragg. "Would you really of shot him?" she asked curiously.

"Who?"

"The redheaded cowhand. Comin' out from under that shelf."

Tragg thought for a moment. "Maybe." He didn't know whether he would have or not.

Jessie looked at him almost as if she were seeing him for the first time. "Do you think they're actually goin' to let us get away?"

"Nothin' much they can do, without horses. We ought to be well on our way to Bosen's Grove by the time they get them rounded up."

Near midmorning they reined up on a knoll to rest the horses and to make sure they were not being followed. Morrasey climbed down from the saddle, took a small bite of tobacco, and gazed off into the distance. After a while he began to hum a grating, unpleasant little tune.

The prisoner seemed not to be interested in escape, so Tragg walked off a few paces and left him alone. "What do you reckon he's thinkin' about?" Jessie asked. "All the men he killed? Or the ones he didn't get to kill?"

Tragg shrugged. He was tired and sour, and the pain in his head radiated to every part of his body.

"You goin' back to bein' a lawman when this is over? If we get out of it, alive?"

The question seemed to surprise him. "It's all I know,"

he said slowly, "except for lecturin'—and I was never any account at that."

"I think you ought to take the lawin' job in El Paso."

Tragg frowned. "Why?"

For the first time her eyes shifted away from his, and she seemed ill at ease. "Maybe it's the men you had a chance to kill and didn't. Even when it looked like the thing to do. And Morrasey . . ." She smiled weakly and made an ineffectual gesture with one hand. "I've been thinkin' about Coly Brown. If it had been Coly you was after, instead of the sodbuster, I'd of been obliged to you for not turnin' him over to that posse."

It seemed to Tragg that this was a curious thing for her to say—a woman who had come such a long way and put herself to so much trouble, for the single purpose of betraying Coly Brown.

Sheriff Max Ellender was sitting up in bed, his splinted leg stiffly out in front of him. He was staring in fascination at his battered deputy. "I got to admit," he said, when Tragg had finished with the story, "that I never had much hope you'd get the sodbuster back alive. Matter of fact, I wasn't too sure you'd make it yourself."

"I wouldn't have if it hadn't been for Miss Ross."

"Miss Ross," Ellender echoed thoughtfully. "Old Valona and two of his pistoleros rode into town this mornin'. Don Carlos is anxious to talk to her about the man that killed his boy. If her story's straight she'll have her bounty money within the next day or so."

"I'll tell her," Tragg said bleakly. He unpinned the deputy's badge and handed it to the sheriff.

189

"Don't reckon you'd be interested in wearin' this as a regular thing, would you?" the sheriff asked. Then he grinned faintly. "No, I guess not, with Jody Barker's widow in the county. Well . . . if there's anything I can do . . ."

They said the usual things. The sheriff bent forward with some difficulty and shook Tragg's hand. Somehow, that rig of tassels and conchos didn't look so ridiculous now. "Good luck. *Hasta la vista.*"

Jessie Ross was sitting on her upturned valise in front of the hotel. She looked at Tragg as he came down the stairs from the sheriff's room. "Southbound stage is due between now and suppertime," she said. "Figgered I might as well wait for it here."

"Valona's in town. Have you talked to him about the bounty?"

"I talked to him." Something about her had changed, but Tragg couldn't say just what it was.

He asked, "Did he give you the money without checking on your story?"

"I didn't give him any story."

Tragg pondered for a moment. "Why not?"

"That's what I've been askin' myself." She laughed—a dry, unmirthful sound. "Don't make much sense, does it? I mean, after all the trouble I went to. And Coly, the shape he's in, is sure to die anyway. Lung fever or Mex pistoleros—what difference does it make?" She sighed. "But when the time came, I couldn't do it."

Tragg sat on the edge of a fire barrel and built a cigarette. "Somehow, I didn't think Coly meant that much to you."

"I was thinkin' about that. It just came to me that I

190

couldn't even recollect what Coly looked like. His face, I mean. I closed my eyes and tried to picture it in my head. But I couldn't. It don't make sense, does it?"

"Maybe it does."

Jessie thought about this for a moment and decided to let it lie. "What about Morrasey?" she asked.

"In jail. There'll be a judge next month to hear his case."

"Will they hang him?"

"Most likely."

"I'm sorry, in a way."

Tragg knew what she meant, but there was nothing anybody could do about it.

She asked, "Are you goin' to try for that lawin' job in El Paso?"

"I guess so. Ellender will put in a word for me, if I need it."

"You think there might be a place for me in El Paso?"

Tragg looked at her—really looked at her—for a moment. He hadn't known many women in his time—still, it was strange that, of the ones he had known, this was the only one he had ever felt truly easy with. "There might be," he said. "We could look."

She looked at him with one eyebrow raised, the only indication that she had noticed anything strange in his use of the word *we*. It might be something for both of them to think about while he went to get his grip—and for some time yet to come.

Center Point Publishing
600 Brooks Road • PO Box 1
Thorndike ME 04986-0001 USA

(207) 568-3717

US & Canada:
1 800 929-9108